I0822153

RETURN TO THE BLACK LAGOON

Return to the Black Lagoon

This is a work of fiction. Names, characters, places, and incidents are products of the author's imagination or have been used fictitiously and are not to be construed as real. Any resemblance to persons, living or dead, actual events, locales, or organizations is coincidental.

ISBN: 979-8-9907254-7-8 (hardback)
979-8-9907254-6-1 (paperback)

Printed in the United States of America

RETURN TO THE BLACK LAGOON

GARY J. ROSE

DEDICATION

To my sister, Debbie Miller, whose keen eye and unwavering support continue to guide my journey through the shadows of classic horror.

After the success of my contemporary re-imaginings of beloved horror films, I stumbled upon a forgotten gem from my youth—a film that, despite its corny charm, once kept me on the edge of my seat in the darkened Hayward theater, soda in hand and popcorn nervously munched. The terror of the gillman lurking just out of sight was as real then as the memories are now.

With Debbie's invaluable editing help, I present this reexamined tale, hoping to recapture that spine-tingling suspense and make you squirm a little in your seat, just as I did all those years ago.

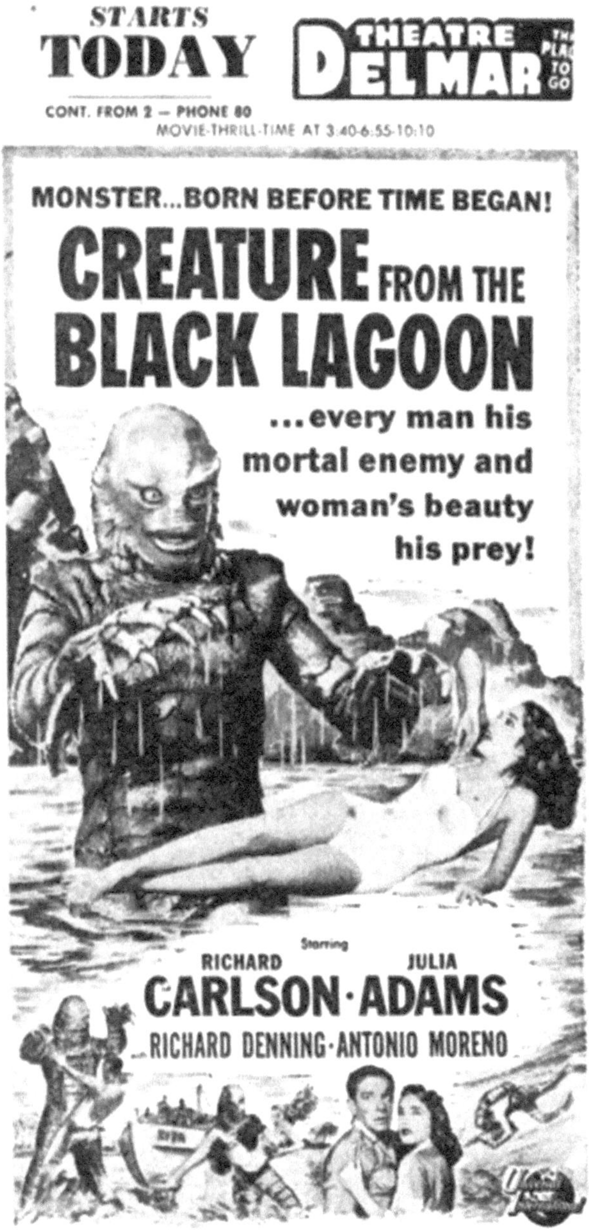
STARTS TODAY
THEATRE DEL MAR
CONT. FROM 2 — PHONE 80
MOVIE-THRILL-TIME AT 3:40-6:55-10:10
MONSTER...BORN BEFORE TIME BEGAN!
CREATURE FROM THE BLACK LAGOON
...every man his mortal enemy and woman's beauty his prey!
Starring
RICHARD CARLSON · JULIA ADAMS
RICHARD DENNING · ANTONIO MORENO

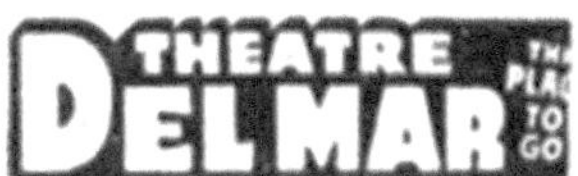

ScriptReader.ai

ScriptReader.ai

HOMAGE

One of the classic horror films of the 1950s was a black-and-white 3D film called *The Creature from the Black Lagoon*. Produced by William Alland and directed by Jack Arnold, the screenplay was written by Harry Essex and Arthur Ross, based on a story by Maurice Zimm. The film stars Richard Carlson, Julia Adams, Richard Denning, Antonio Moreno, Nestor Paiva, and Whit Bissell.

The plot follows a group of scientists who encounter a piscine amphibious humanoid in the waters of the Amazon. The Creature, also known as the Gill-man, was portrayed by Ben Chapman on land and by Ricou Browning underwater. Produced and distributed by Universal-International, *Creature from the Black Lagoon* premiered in Detroit on February 12, 1954, and was released regionally on various dates.

The film was shot in three dimensions (3D) and originally projected using the polarized light method. Audience members wore viewers with gray polarizing filters, similar to those used today. Because the 1950s 3D film fad had peaked in mid-1953 and was fading by early 1954, many audiences saw the film "flat," in two dimensions (2D). Typically, the film was shown in 3D in large downtown theaters and flat in smaller neighborhood theaters. In 1975, *Creature from the Black Lagoon* was re-released in the red-and-blue-glasses anaglyph 3D format, which was also used for a 1980 home video release on Beta and VHS videocassettes.

The story begins with a geology expedition in the Amazon uncovering fossilized evidence from the Devonian period (a skeletal hand with webbed fingers) that links land and sea animals. Expedition leader Dr. Carl Maia visits the marine biology institute to reunite with ichthyologist Dr. David Reed, who persuades his boss, Dr. Mark Williams, to fund a return expedition to search for the rest of the skeleton.

The team, which includes David's girlfriend and colleague Kay Lawrence, Dr. Edwin Thompson, and the crusty captain Lucas, returns to the Amazon only to find Carl's assistants killed. Lucas attributes their deaths to a jaguar, but the team is unsure. A further excavation yields no new findings, but David suggests the embankment containing the rest of the skeleton might have fallen into the water and been carried downriver, leading them to the "Black Lagoon," a place Lucas describes as a paradise from which no one has returned.

The Creature, intrigued by the beautiful Kay, follows the team to the Black Lagoon. Various encounters with the Creature result in deaths and attacks, ultimately leading to its capture and escape. The film culminates with the Creature abducting Kay and being pursued by the team, who rescue her and fatally wound the Creature, which retreats into the lagoon.

Creature from the Black Lagoon spawned two sequels: *Revenge of the Creature* (1955), also filmed and released in 3D in an attempt to revive the format, and *The Creature Walks Among Us* (1956), filmed in 2D. Before the release of the second film, the Creature made a comedic appearance with Abbott and Costello on an episode of *The Colgate Comedy Hour*, commonly referred to as *Abbott and Costello Meet the Creature from the Black Lagoon*.

However, Hollywood has shown little enthusiasm for these earlier sequels and has expressed interest in a contemporary script that reimagines the original. To date, no producer or screenwriter has successfully pitched a production company.

This novel pays homage to the original film, similar to my reimaginings of other horror classics like *House on Haunted Hill Resurrection*, *The Tingler*, *Carnival of Lost Souls*, and *The Birds Return*.

CHAPTER 1

Dr. Sarah Blake woke in her tent, drenched in sweat from the hot Amazonian sun, even though it was just daybreak. The cacophony of the Amazon forest greeted her ears—chirping birds, buzzing insects, and the distant calls of monkeys. She stretched and realized her pillow was also wet, along with her white t-shirt and panties. "Ugh. What I do for science," she thought, grabbing a towel from her suitcase to dry herself off.

Sarah, in her early 30s, was a striking woman with blonde hair that framed her face in loose waves and piercing blue eyes that reflected her intelligence and determination. Her athletic build and sun-kissed skin spoke of countless hours spent in the field. Despite the challenging conditions, her natural beauty shone through, making her an attractive figure in the scientific community. She took a deep breath, ready to face another day of exploration and discovery in the heart of the Amazon.

There was no need to replace her t-shirt since the heat and humidity would soon soak her with sweat again. She removed her panties and put on a fresh pair, followed by cargo shorts. Grabbing her straw hat, she unzipped the tent's opening and stepped out into the vibrant symphony of the Amazon.

She took a deep breath, filling her lungs with the rich, earthy scent of the rainforest. The day promised more exploration and discovery, and she was ready to face whatever challenges awaited in the heart of this untamed wilderness.

"Good morning, Doctor," Miguel, the expedition guide, called out as soon as he saw Sarah exit her tent. "I have breakfast almost ready."

"Thank you, Miguel. How about some coffee? Is that ready?"

"Sí, señorita... I mean, Doctor. The coffee is ready," he replied with a sheepish grin, correcting himself.

Sarah chuckled. "It's okay, Miguel. You can call me Sarah when it's just us. Doctor Blake sounds too formal out here."

Miguel nodded, his eyes twinkling with amusement. "As you wish, Sarah. But you know, respect is important, even in the jungle."

She smiled, appreciating his dedication and respect. "I do know, and I appreciate it. But a little informality won't hurt. Now, let's see about that coffee."

Miguel handed her a steaming cup of coffee, the rich aroma mingling with the earthy scents of the forest. Sarah took a sip, savoring the warmth and flavor. "Perfect. Just what I needed to start the day."

"Anything for you, Doct— I mean, Sarah," Miguel said, giving her a friendly nod before turning back to his cooking.

Sarah joined the rest of the group gathered around a makeshift picnic table constructed from fallen tree branches. At the head of the table sat Captain Jose Delgado of the River Queen, a portly sixty-year-old with a sweat-drenched white long-sleeved shirt and tan pants, chomping on an unlit cigar. His presence commanded respect, and his gruff demeanor was softened by a twinkle of humor in his eyes.

To his right was Dr. Emily Carter, a geologist who realized how much she hated the Amazon as soon as the River Queen left the docks. Constantly spraying herself with mosquito repellent and swatting at flies, Emily's frustration was palpable. Sarah often wondered if she would last the duration of the expedition, given her visible discomfort.

Next to Emily was Dr. Alan Richards, a renowned ichthyologist but also, in Sarah's opinion, an insufferable egotist. In recent years, Richards had allowed his scientific pursuits to take a backseat to his quest for fame and fortune. Yet, coming from a wealthy family and funding the entire expedition, he was a necessary evil. Sarah tolerated his insolence, knowing their research depended on his financial support.

Finally, there was Dr. Brad Freeman, the last member of their team and Sarah's love interest for the past six months. At thirty-six, Brad was tall, dark, and handsome, embodying the ideal image of a rugged scientist. He had overruled Richards' objections, who believed that having two women aboard the boat was inviting trouble. Brad's steadfast support and quiet confidence had endeared him to Sarah, and their budding romance added a layer of warmth to the grueling expedition.

"How did you sleep, Sarah?" Brad asked, scooting over to make room for her at the table.

"Actually, not bad once I got used to the sounds of the jungle at night," Sarah replied, settling down beside him. "A couple of times, though, I shot up in fright and grabbed my flashlight."

Captain Delgado laughed heartily. "Yes, señorita, the jungle has many new noises that come out at night. But it is the things that you cannot hear that you should be worried about."

"What things?" Dr. Carter asked, her face paling with concern.

"Oh, there are many venomous snakes out at night, as well as foot-long centipedes," Delgado explained, his tone both serious and teasing. "Probably the worst, however, would be the jaguars. They are very quick and silent, but normally they stay away from humans."

Emily's eyes widened as she glanced around nervously. "Jaguars? Really?"

"Yes, really," Delgado confirmed, his face softening with a reassuring smile. "But do not worry, Dr. Carter. Jaguars are elusive creatures. They prefer to avoid humans unless provoked or very hungry."

Brad placed a comforting hand on Emily's arm. "We'll be fine, Emily. We're taking all the necessary precautions."

Sarah nodded in agreement. "And we have Captain Delgado. He knows these parts better than anyone."

Delgado puffed out his chest with a modest pride. "Indeed, I have been navigating these waters for over thirty years. Trust me, you are in good hands."

Emily took a deep breath, trying to relax. "Thanks, Captain. I guess it just takes some getting used to."

Sarah leaned in closer to Brad, whispering, "I think we'll all be a bit jumpy until we get our jungle legs."

Brad chuckled softly, squeezing her hand. "We're scientists, right? Adaptation is part of the job." The group shared a light laugh, the tension easing as they continued their breakfast, surrounded by the sounds and sights of the untamed Amazon.

"So, Doctor Richards, you are paying good money for me to navigate the River Queen into rarely visited parts of the Amazon. What exactly are you looking for?"

CHAPTER 2

Richards leaned back in his chair, gazing out at the horizon. The sun climbing towards its zenith, casting long shadows over the gently rolling waves. The rest of the team, still buzzing with the thrill of their discovery, fell silent as he began to speak.

"Dr. Blake wasn't always the cautious woman you see today," Richards began, a nostalgic smile playing on his lips. "There was a time, years ago, when her curiosity led her into the heart of untamed wilderness, far from the safety of our modern world."

He paused, letting the weight of his words settle over the group. "It was in those early days, during one of her first expeditions to South America, that Blake stumbled upon something truly extraordinary. In a remote jungle, where the trees grew so thick they blotted out the sky, she found a cave. And in that cave, she discovered fossils that defied everything we thought we knew about prehistory."

Richards' eyes sparkled with the memory. "These fossils were unlike any she had ever seen. They were of creatures that seemed to belong to a time long before the dinosaurs we know today. Massive, serpentine skeletons with features that suggested a lineage stretching back hundreds of millions of years, to a time when the world was a very different place."

The team leaned in closer, captivated. "Blake spent weeks in that cave, meticulously cataloging every bone, every fragment. But it wasn't just the fossils that were remarkable. The cave walls were covered in ancient carvings, depicting scenes of these creatures in their prime. It was as if she had stumbled upon a lost history, a window into a world that had been forgotten by time."

Richards took a deep breath, his voice growing softer. "But as she delved deeper, Blake realized something else. The cave wasn't just a tomb for these ancient beasts; it was a gateway. A gateway to understanding how life on this planet had evolved, how creatures had adapted and survived through cataclysmic changes."

He looked around at the team, their faces reflecting a mixture of awe and curiosity. "Blake's discovery rewrote the history books, and it changed her. She became more cautious, more aware of the fragile balance of life. And it was that awareness that led her to our current expedition, to find the source of these mysteries and uncover the truths hidden beneath the waves."

Richards' voice trailed off, leaving the team in contemplative silence. The sun had dipped below the horizon, and the first stars began to twinkle in the evening sky.

"Alright," Richards said, standing up and stretching. "It's time we reboarded the boat and continued our journey. We've got a lot of ground—or rather, water—to cover before we reach our next destination."

"Captain Delgado, you have been on the river most of your life. Have you heard stories about an ancient civilization living in the area we are heading too?" Sarah asked, causing everyone to turn and focus on the captain.

"Your Hollywood sometimes exaggerates about the dangers here in the Amazon, like that movie about the giant Anaconda. It made for a good story, no? But there are no snakes out here that big or smart enough to take on a boat full of people. This river will sting you, bite you, and yes, if given the chance, eat you." Emily shook trying to escape what Captain Delgado was saying.

As they walked back to the boat, he continued to speak, now about the local legends of the Amazon. "This river has its fair share of stories and myths. The locals believe it to be a place of magic and danger, filled with creatures and spirits that protect the jungle."

He pointed to the dense foliage along the riverbank. "Take the legend of the Yacuruna, for example. They're said to be powerful water spirits that can transform into human form. They live in underwater cities and lure unsuspecting people into their domain, never to be seen again."

The team shivered slightly, the shadows of the jungle closing in around them. Delgado continued, his tone serious. "Then there's the tale of El Tunche, a vengeful spirit that roams the forest at night. It's said that if you hear its eerie whistle, you should run the other way, for it means death is near."

They reached the boat and began to board, but the captain wasn't finished. "And of course, there's the story of the Mapinguari, a giant, ape-like creature with a single eye and a mouth on its belly. It's rumored to be a guardian of the forest, attacking anyone who dares to harm the jungle."

As the boat set off and the Captain begins to guide the boat he lowered his voice. "But the most chilling legend of all is that of the Gillman. According to local lore, it's a half-human, half-fish creature that lives in the darkest depths of the Amazon. It's said to be incredibly intelligent and fiercely territorial, attacking anyone who ventures too close to its lair."

The team exchanged uneasy glances, the weight of the stories settling over them. The boat cut through the darkening waters, the sense of adventure and discovery hanging thick in the air, promising more secrets to be unveiled in the days to come.

As the boat glided silently through the winding waterways of the Amazon, the dense jungle seemed to close in around them. The air was thick with humidity, and the rich scent of earth and vegetation filled their lungs. Towering trees with sprawling canopies blocked out much of the sky, creating a world of green shadows and dappled sunlight.

Birds of every imaginable color darted through the trees, their calls a cacophony of life. Scarlet macaws, with their brilliant red, yellow, and blue feathers, squawked and preened in the branches above. Tiny hummingbirds flitted past, their wings a blur as they hovered over vibrant flowers, sipping nectar. Occasionally, a harpy eagle could be seen soaring high above, its massive wings casting a fleeting shadow over the boat.

The stillness of the river was deceptive. Just beneath the surface, unseen eyes watched their every move. Caimans, part of the alligator family, lay in wait along the riverbanks. These ambush predators were masters of camouflage, their rough, scaly hides blending seamlessly with the muddy water and vegetation. Like their crocodilian relatives, caimans were patient hunters, waiting for unsuspecting animals to come and drink from the Amazon River and its tributaries.

Richards pointed out a particularly large caiman basking in the sun on a fallen log. Its eyes, dark and unblinking, followed their progress with a cold intelligence. "They can remain motionless for hours," he explained. "But the moment prey gets within reach, they strike with incredible speed and force."

The team watched in awe as a capybara, the world's largest rodent, cautiously approached the water's edge. Unaware of the danger lurking nearby, it lowered its head to drink. Suddenly, the caiman exploded from the water, its powerful jaws closing around the capybara with a bone-crushing snap. The struggle was brief, and the caiman dragged its prey back into the murky depths.

"Nature can be brutal," Richards said quietly, the team absorbing the raw display of survival. "But it's also incredibly fascinating. Everything here has adapted perfectly to its environment."

As the boat glided silently through the winding waterways of the Amazon, the dense jungle seemed to close in around them. The air was thick with humidity, and the rich scent of earth and vegetation filled their lungs. Towering trees with sprawling canopies blocked out much of the sky, creating a world of green shadows and dappled sunlight.

The stillness of the river was deceptive. Just beneath the surface, unseen eyes watched their every move. Caimans, part of the alligator family, lay in wait along the riverbanks. These ambush predators were masters of camouflage, their rough, scaly hides blending seamlessly with the muddy water and vegetation. Like their crocodilian relatives, caimans were patient hunters, waiting for unsuspecting animals to come and drink from the Amazon River and its tributaries.

CHAPTER 3

The further they traveled, the more the jungle seemed to come alive around them. Brightly colored frogs clung to tree trunks, their skin warning of deadly toxins. Monkeys swung from branch to branch, chattering noisily as they passed overhead. Occasionally, they caught glimpses of elusive jaguars moving stealthily through the underbrush, their spotted coats blending perfectly with the dappled light.

The cacophony of jungle noises was suddenly interrupted by the piercing, blood-curdling sound of Emily's screams. Everyone turned in her direction and saw a large snake hanging from the roof of the boat, hissing menacingly at her. Before anyone could react, Captain Delgado, still chomping on his cigar, grabbed the snake by the throat and flung it overboard, where it swiftly swam away.

Sarah rushed over and hugged Emily, who was still in shock. "What if it had bitten me?" Emily stammered. "It could have killed me with its poison."

Captain Delgado smiled reassuringly. "No, senorita. That snake was not a poisonous one. It was a boa constrictor. It probably fell onto the roof from a tree where it was hunting birds or monkeys."

Emily's breathing began to steady as she processed his words. "A boa constrictor?" she repeated, her voice trembling slightly. "But it was so big."

Delgado nodded. "They can grow quite large, but they are not venomous. They kill by constriction, wrapping around their prey and squeezing tightly. You were never in real danger from its bite."

Sarah gently stroked Emily's hair, trying to comfort her. "It's okay, Emily. We're safe now."

Captain Delgado chuckled and took another puff from his cigar. "Welcome to the jungle, ladies. Always expect the unexpected out here."

The boat resumed its journey through the dense, vibrant landscape of the Amazon, the incident with the snake a stark reminder of the wild, untamed world they were venturing into. The team remained alert, their senses heightened by the sudden encounter, ready for whatever surprises the jungle might have in store next.

The team felt a sense of profound wonder and respect for the untamed beauty of the Amazon. The journey was not just a passage through a physical landscape but a voyage into a world where every creature, plant, and river had a story to tell. As the boat pushed onward, the mysteries of the jungle beckoned, promising adventure and discovery with each bend of the river.

"How much longer, Delgado?" an impatient Richards asked, wiping sweat from his brow. "It looks like this river is getting narrower and narrower."

Before the captain could answer, Sarah pointed to a bend in the river. "I think it's just beyond this twist in the river." Captain Delgado slowed down the River Queen, allowing the boat to gently glide around the point.

"Yes, there's the camp," Sarah announced to everyone. "Wait! Something is wrong. The main hut looks like it is destroyed."

"It could have been a bad storm," Brad chimed in, walking over to Sarah and placing his arm around her waist. Captain Delgado skillfully docked the River Queen as close to the shore as possible, but the dense undergrowth and tangle of underwater roots required the team to take two rowboats to transport themselves and their gear to the camp.

As they paddled towards the shore, the closer they got, the more the damage became apparent. The main hut's roof was partially caved in, and several smaller structures lay in shambles. The air was thick with the smell of damp wood and vegetation, mixed with the faint, lingering scent of smoke.

"What could have caused this?" Emily wondered aloud, her voice tinged with concern.

"Could be anything," Delgado replied. "Storms, wild animals, or even human interference. We won't know until we take a closer look."

Once they reached the shore, the team disembarked and began unloading their equipment. The camp, which had once been a bustling hub of activity, now looked abandoned and forlorn. Richards, Sarah, Brad, Emily, and Captain Delgado, and the two deckhands moved cautiously towards the damaged huts, scanning their surroundings for any signs of recent activity.

"Spread out and check the area," Richards instructed. "Look for any clues as to what happened here."

Sarah and Brad moved towards the main hut, stepping over fallen beams and debris. Inside, they found overturned furniture, scattered supplies, and signs of a hasty departure. It was clear that whatever had happened, it had caused the inhabitants to leave in a hurry.

One of the deck hands called out to Captain Delgado very agitated. Delgado quickly examined his find and called out to the rest.

"Richards, over here!" Delgado called out, pointing to a set of muddy footprints leading away from the camp and into the jungle.

Richards knelt down to inspect the prints. "These are fresh. Whoever left them can't be far."

Meanwhile, Emily and Captain Delgado examined the other huts, finding similar scenes of chaos and abandonment. "Looks like everyone left in a hurry," Delgado observed, his eyes scanning the tree line.

Richards stood up, his expression determined. "We'll set up our camp here and then follow these tracks as far as they take us. If there are survivors out there, we need to find them."

As the team began to organize their gear and set up camp, the weight of their new mission settled over them. The jungle, with all its mysteries and dangers, was closing in around them, and they knew that the answers they sought lay somewhere within its depths.

Emily asked if she could stay at the camp site since the heat was really affecting here. Richards looked at both Emily and Brad and both nodded. "I think that would be a good idea, Emily. We should return shortly after nightfall.

Captain Delgado and his two deckhands returned to the River Queen to rest. They chuckled among themselves about the "gringos" heading out in the heat of the day to follow tracks. As Delgado settled into a chair, he called out to Richards and the others, who were preparing to head into the jungle.

"Listen up!" Delgado shouted. "Be careful when you cross the smaller tributaries. This time of day, the piranhas are especially active. They can strip a man to the bone in minutes if you're not careful."

He paused, his expression serious. "And watch out for other dangers. The jungle is full of surprises—poisonous snakes, spiders, and who knows what else. Stay alert and stick together. Don't take unnecessary risks."

The team nodded, taking in Delgado's warning. Richards gave a quick thumbs-up to the captain before turning back to his group. "You heard him, everyone. Let's move cautiously and stay on our guard."

With that, Captain Delgado watched as the team disappeared into the dense foliage, his earlier amusement replaced by a flicker of concern. The jungle was no place for complacency, and he knew all too well the dangers that lurked just out of sight. He relit his cigar, the orange ember glowing brightly in the dimming light, and grabbed a beer from the boat's refrigerator, taking a long, reflective sip.

The deckhands continued their light-hearted banter, oblivious to the growing tension that clung to the humid air. The sounds of the jungle seemed to grow louder, more insistent, as if warning of unseen perils lurking in the shadows.

As the River Queen bobbed gently in the water, no one onboard noticed the small, almost imperceptible bubbles rising to the surface along the side of the vessel. The water's calm surface was disturbed only slightly, the ripples fading quickly in the fading light.

Delgado took another sip of his beer, his gaze drifting over the river's edge. He felt a nagging unease, a sense that something was not quite right. The jungle, usually a cacophony of noise, seemed to hold its breath, the sudden silence broken only by the occasional splash of a fish or the distant call of a bird.

The deckhands, still chuckling, failed to see the dark shapes gliding silently beneath the water, their movements deliberate and slow. The bubbles increased slightly in number, forming a small, frothy patch that clung to the boat's hull.

Delgado's eyes narrowed as he glanced at the horizon, the sun dipping lower, casting long shadows over the river. He couldn't shake the feeling that they were being watched, that the jungle itself was keeping a wary eye on their every move.

The air grew heavier, more oppressive, as the last rays of sunlight slipped away. The boat creaked softly, a sound that seemed unnaturally loud in the gathering dusk. Delgado's fingers tightened around his beer bottle, his instincts honed by years in the wild urging him to stay vigilant.

"Captain Delgado," Emily called out from the camp. "Would it be alright if I joined you and your crew on the boat until the rest of them return?"

Sliding his cigar from one side of his mouth to the other and glancing at his crew, he smiled. "Si, señorita. But you have both row boats, so you will have to row to us."

"Okay. I think I can do that. Just a minute," she replied as she grabbed a flashlight.

Emily's heart pounded as she began rowing toward the River Queen, the beam of her flashlight cutting through the inky darkness. Unbeknownst to her, a pair of unblinking eyes watched her every move. The creature, intrigued by the unfolding event, silently lowered itself into the water. It swam upside down just beneath the surface, its shadow mirroring the silhouette of the boat stride for stride.

With a sudden, deliberate motion, the creature struck the underside of the boat. The impact sent a jolt through Emily, causing her to lose her grip on the oars. Panic surged through her as the boat rocked violently. She let out a terrified scream, her voice echoing across the stillness of the night. "Captain Delgado! Something hit the boat!"

Captain Delgado, standing on the deck of the River Queen, leaned over the railing, his calm demeanor a stark contrast to Emily's fear. He used the boats powerful lamp to light up the river but saw nothing. "It's alright, Emily," he called out reassuringly. "You probably just hit a tree root. Keep going; you're almost here."

Emily tried to steady her breathing, her eyes darting nervously around the water's surface, searching for any sign of what lurked beneath. She gripped the oars tightly, her knuckles white, and resumed rowing, her heart pounding even louder in her chest. Beneath the boat, the creature continued to swim, its eyes gleaming with a predatory delight as it watched her struggle.

Yet, despite his growing unease, the captain couldn't pinpoint the source of his discomfort. The jungle held its secrets close, revealing nothing, but hinting at everything. And as the night began to fall, the River Queen lay at anchor, a solitary vessel in a vast, unknowable wilderness, surrounded by unseen eyes and hidden dangers.

CHAPTER 4

Sarah, Brad, and Richards, using the light from a full moon, cautiously followed the footprints that led away from the destroyed camp. The moonlight filtered through the dense canopy above, casting eerie shadows on the ground. The air was thick with the scent of damp earth and the distant call of unseen birds.

Sarah, her face set with determination, glanced at Brad, who walked beside her, his eyes scanning the path ahead. Richards, the team leader, walked slightly ahead, his sharp gaze following the trail of the creature.

"Stay close and keep your eyes open," Richards murmured, his voice a low rumble. "We don't know what we're dealing with here."

"Look," and excited Richards calls out. Using the beam of his flashlight he pointed it towards several impression in the ground. "These footprints are huge and look at the claws."

"And look in-between the claws. It looks like webbing like you see on duck feet," Sarah added. Each step they took seemed to amplify the sense of dread that hung in the air. The group moved cautiously, their senses on high alert.

Suddenly, a loud splash echoed from the nearby lagoon, causing all three to stop in their tracks. Sarah's heart leapt into her throat as she gripped her flashlight tighter.

"What was that?" Brad whispered, his voice trembling slightly.

"Probably just a fish," Richards said, though his eyes darted nervously toward the water. "Or maybe one of those legends Captain Delgado mentioned. You know, the ones about creatures lurking in these waters."

Sarah couldn't help but shiver at the thought. The stories Delgado had shared the night before were chilling, filled with ancient myths and unexplained disappearances. Another splash sounded, closer this time, followed by a faint ripple on the water's surface. The creature was toying with them, its presence a constant, unseen menace.

They pressed on, their footsteps silent on the forest floor. As they ventured deeper into the jungle, Sarah began to notice subtle changes in their surroundings. The lush greenery gave way to strange, twisted plants that seemed out of place. The air grew heavier, the light dimmer. The rock formations, once familiar and modern, now appeared ancient and weathered, as if they had stepped back in time.

"I think we need to turn back Alan," Sarah suggested.

"Look at this," Brad said, pointing to a peculiar plant with broad, spiked leaves. "This doesn't belong here. It looks prehistoric."

Richards nodded, his expression grim. "We're definitely not in Kansas anymore. Keep moving but stay alert. The landscape is changing, and I don't like it either Emily. Just a few more minutes.

The group continued, the sense of unease growing with each step. The splashes had ceased, but the silence that followed was even more unnerving. Sarah could feel the weight of something gazing upon them, an invisible predator stalking its prey. She exchanged a worried glance with Brad, who offered a reassuring nod.

They reached a clearing where the ground was littered with ancient, fossilized rocks. The air was thick with the scent of something primordial, something untouched by time. Richards crouched to examine one of the footprints, his brow furrowing in concentration.

"Lets pick up as many rocks as we can and take them back to Emily to analyze," Richards said, while examining the tracks.

"These tracks," he said slowly, "they're leading us somewhere. Somewhere important."

Sarah took a deep breath, steeling herself for whatever lay ahead. The jungle around them seemed to pulse with life, an echo of a time long forgotten. They were on the creature's trail, but the journey was fraught with danger and uncertainty. The prehistoric landscape around them was a stark reminder of how out of their depth they truly were.

As they moved forward, the sense of being watched grew stronger. The creature was close, its presence a constant, unseen threat. The jungle seemed to close in around them, the ancient trees and rocks a silent testament to the passage of time. Sarah knew they had to stay vigilant, for the creature could strike at any moment. The path ahead was uncertain, but they had no choice but to follow it, wherever it might lead.

Sarah knelt down to examine a particularly large fossil using her flashlight, her fingers tracing the ancient patterns etched into the stone. Suddenly, a movement above caught her eye. She looked up just in time to see a giant snake slithering down from a tree branch, its scales glistening in the dappled sunlight. Sarah, who had been standing nearby, let out a piercing scream as the snake hissed, its tongue flicking in and out menacingly.

"Move! Get back!" Richards shouted, drawing his knife and stepping between the snake and the team.

The snake coiled, ready to strike, its eyes fixed on the intruders.

"Alan... enough," Brad said sternly, pulling Sarah back and away from the danger. "We need to get out of here and come back tomorrow. This place is too dangerous."

Richards hesitated, his eyes still on the snake. Then, with a reluctant nod, he backed away, signaling the others to follow. The group retreated cautiously, their nerves frayed and hearts pounding. The jungle seemed to close in around them as they made their way back to the safety of the camp, the sense of being watched never leaving them. The creature, the snake, and the unsettling changes in the environment had all served as stark reminders that they were intruding on a world that did not welcome them. They would return, but only after regrouping and reassessing their approach.

Pulling itself out of the water, the creature moved stealthily, using the thick fauna as cover to watch the three humans retrace their path back to their camp. Its eyes, gleaming with a predatory intelligence, followed their every move. Among the trio, the creature was particularly fascinated with Sarah, her fearful demeanor captivating its primal instincts.

As the group disappeared into the dense foliage, the same giant snake that had threatened Sarah earlier slithered down from a nearby tree, its eyes locked on the creature. With a sudden, swift strike, the snake lunged at the creature. The creature reacted with lightning speed, its powerful claws swiping through the air. In a single, decisive motion, it decapitated the snake, the severed head falling to the ground with a dull thud.

The creature reached down, grabbing the still-twisting body of the snake. It lifted the carcass to its mouth, tearing into the flesh with sharp teeth. Blood dripped from its jaws as it devoured the snake, savoring the taste of its fresh kill. With each bite, the creature's focus never wavered from the direction of the humans' retreat.

Once it had consumed its meal, the creature slipped back into the water, moving silently and effortlessly. It swam with purpose, its mind fixated on the strange beings that had invaded its territory. The encounter with Sarah had ignited a spark of curiosity and hunger within it, a dangerous combination for anyone who dared to venture near the black lagoon.

The creature's movements were fluid and stealthy, its body a shadow beneath the surface. It returned to the safety of the river, blending seamlessly into its environment. But its thoughts lingered on Sarah, and the creature's fascination with her would undoubtedly lead to further encounters, each more perilous than the last.

CHAPTER 5

Upon their return, Emily rowed back to shore as Captain Delgado called out to them. "Any luck?"

"Yes!" an excited Richards replied. "We found a whole outcropping of fossils. There's an area back there where time seems to have stopped. Even the jungle shifts to a prehistoric period. Just add a few dinosaurs and we would have our own Jurassic Park."

Captain Delgado immediately made the sign of the cross. "Jesus, Mr. Richards. Be careful what you wish for."

Richards waved him off, a broad grin on his face, as he showed the fossils and rocks to a very interested Emily. The excitement in his voice was palpable as he described their discoveries. Emily leaned in, examining the ancient remnants with wide-eyed fascination.

As they marveled at the fossils, a sudden splash echoed from the water behind them. Emily's heart skipped a beat, her eyes darting to the dark surface of the lagoon. The ripples spread out, and for a moment, she could have sworn she saw a shadow moving just beneath the water.

"Did you hear that?" she whispered, her voice tinged with unease.

Richards glanced over his shoulder, his expression dismissive. "Probably just a fish. Or maybe those legends Delgado keeps talking about."

Captain Delgado's face remained stern, his eyes scanning the water with a wary look. "Legends or not, we need to stay vigilant. This place is full of surprises, and not all of them are pleasant."

Sarah nodded, feeling a chill run down her spine. The creature's earlier encounter and the eerie transformation of the jungle still fresh in her mind. She couldn't shake the feeling that they were being watched, that something ancient and dangerous lurked in the shadows.

As they gathered their findings and prepared to turn in for the night, Emily couldn't help but cast one last glance at the water. The surface was calm now, but she knew better than to trust appearances. The lagoon held many secrets, and they had only just begun to uncover them. She leans into Sarah.

"Would it be possible for me to share your tent tonight? I don't know what has gotten into me, but this place frightens the beJesus out of me," Emily asked, her voice trembling slightly.

Sarah looked up from her gear, her expression softening with understanding. "Sure, Emily, and I promise not to snore," she replied with a wink.

Emily's initial shock at Sarah's response quickly melted away when she saw the huge smile spreading across her friend's face. The warmth and humor in Sarah's eyes were a welcome relief after the day's unsettling events. Emily managed a weak laugh, feeling a bit of the tension ease from her shoulders.

"Thanks, Sarah. I don't know what I'd do without you," Emily said, her gratitude evident in her tone.

"Hey, that's what friends are for," Sarah replied, giving Emily a reassuring pat on the back. "We'll get through this together, no matter what creepy legends or prehistoric jungles throw at us."

As they settled into the tent, the sounds of the night seemed to grow louder, the rustling leaves and distant animal calls a constant reminder of the unknown lurking outside. Emily lay down, her heart still racing from the day's events. But with Sarah's presence beside her, she felt a bit more secure, ready to face whatever challenges the mysterious lagoon had in store for them.

The next morning, Captain Delgado had his deckhands prepare breakfast for the scientists. The scent of brewing coffee mingled with the crisp morning air, drawing Brad out of his tent. He stretched and inhaled deeply, savoring the aroma. Moments later, Richards emerged, rubbing the sleep from his eyes.

"You know, Alan," Brad said thoughtfully as he poured himself a cup of coffee, "I've been thinking about what might be at the bottom of this spot we're at. There could be fossils down there even older than the ones we gathered yesterday."

Richards nodded, his interest piqued. "That's not a bad idea. There's no telling what we might find. Let's you and I dive down right after breakfast. Emily and Sarah have enough fossils to examine while we're gone."

Brad smiled, the prospect of uncovering more ancient relics exciting him. "Sounds like a plan. We should prepare our diving gear and make sure everything is in order."

As they discussed their plan, Emily and Sarah joined them, drawn by the smell of breakfast. Captain Delgado handed them plates of scrambled eggs and bacon, and they all sat down to eat.

"What's the plan for today?" Emily asked, looking from Brad to Richards.

"We're thinking of diving to the bottom of this spot," Brad explained. "There could be even older fossils down there, and we want to see what we can find. You and Sarah can continue examining the ones we collected yesterday."

Emily nodded, her curiosity piqued. "That sounds exciting. Be careful down there."

"We will," Richards assured her. "We'll take all necessary precautions."

After finishing their breakfast, Brad and Richards gathered their diving equipment. They checked their oxygen tanks, tested their masks, and ensured their wetsuits were secure. The morning sun glinted off the water as they prepared to dive, the anticipation building.

Emily and Sarah watched as the two men descended into the depths, their forms gradually disappearing into the dark water. The surface rippled for a moment before becoming still again, leaving the women alone with their thoughts and the task at hand.

As Emily examined one of the fossils, she couldn't shake the feeling of unease that had settled over her since the previous day. The jungle, the creature, and now the mysterious depths of the lagoon all seemed to be connected in ways they had yet to understand. She glanced at Sarah, who was meticulously cataloging their findings.

"Let's hope they find something extraordinary," Sarah said with a smile, breaking the silence.

"Yeah," Emily replied, forcing a smile. "Let's hope." The minutes ticked by slowly as they waited for Brad and Richards to return, the sense of anticipation and anxiety growing with each passing moment.

On the shoreline opposite the position of the River Queen, the creature watched intently as Richards and Brad prepared to lower themselves into the water. The morning light glinted off their strange equipment, piquing the creature's curiosity and wariness. As they submerged, it observed the stream of bubbles rising to the surface, now realizing their intent to enter its domain.

With calculated silence, the creature slid into the water, barely making a splash. It moved swiftly, its powerful body cutting through the murky depths with ease. The creature descended ahead of Richards and Brad, its keen senses guiding it to a concealed position among the dense weeds and tangled roots of the Amazonian floor.

The underwater world was a realm of shadows and flickering light, the perfect environment for the creature to blend in. It positioned itself strategically, its eyes fixed on the two intruders who dared to invade its territory. The creature's muscles tensed, ready to strike if necessary, but for now, it remained hidden, watching and waiting.

Richards and Brad descended deeper, their flashlights cutting narrow beams through the dark water. They were oblivious to the danger lurking nearby, focused solely on the potential discoveries that lay ahead. The further they went, the thicker the vegetation became, the roots and weeds creating an almost impenetrable barrier.

Richards paused to examine a cluster of ancient-looking rocks, unaware of the creature's gaze upon him. Brad floated nearby, his attention divided between the underwater landscape and the limited visibility.

As they continued their exploration, the creature shifted slightly, its presence causing a faint ripple in the water. Richards felt a chill run down his spine, a sense of foreboding that he couldn't quite place. He glanced around, his eyes straining to see beyond the reach of his flashlight.

"Brad," he signaled through their underwater communication system, "keep an eye out. Something doesn't feel right. I thought a saw a large animal or fish over there."

Brad nodded, tightening his grip on his equipment. The two men moved cautiously, the eerie silence of the depths only amplifying their growing unease. Every movement, every shadow seemed to hide potential danger.

Unseen by the men, the creature slowly edged closer, its predatory instincts sharp and ready. It observed their every move, its mind calculating the best moment to reveal itself. The underwater realm was its territory, and it would defend it fiercely if provoked.

As Richards and Brad continued their search, the suspense in the water was palpable. The unseen threat loomed large, and the boundary between hunter and prey grew increasingly blurred. They were strangers in a perilous world, and the creature was determined to ensure they never forgot it.

CHAPTER 6

Brad and Richards carefully collected the fossils they wanted to bring to the surface, their hands moving methodically despite the eerie silence of the underwater world. Each fossil they unearthed was a testament to the ancient past, and their excitement momentarily eclipsed the underlying tension.

Brad's heart pounded as he examined a particularly well-preserved specimen, his mind racing with thoughts of the incredible discovery they were making. Suddenly, out of the corner of his eye, he saw a dark shape moving swiftly from a cluster of tree roots to another hidden location among the dense vegetation. His blood ran cold.

Panic surged through him, and he pointed frantically at the spot where he had seen the creature. His eyes were wide with fear as he signaled to Richards.

"There! Did you see that?" his gestures screamed, though the underwater environment muffled their communication to mere signals and expressions.

Richards turned quickly, his flashlight beam cutting through the murky water. He strained to see what had terrified Brad but found nothing but shadows and swirling debris. The eerie stillness of the underwater jungle seemed to mock their presence.

Brad's panic was palpable, and Richards, sensing the urgency, motioned for him to remain calm. He signaled for them to surface slowly, his movements deliberate and composed. Brad nodded, swallowing his fear, and together they began their ascent.

As they rose through the water, their eyes remained fixed on the depths below, searching for any sign of the creature Brad had seen. The water around them felt colder, the weight of the unknown pressing heavily on their minds.

Brad's thoughts raced, replaying the sight of the dark shape moving with predatory grace. He couldn't shake the image from his mind, the sheer size and speed of the creature unlike anything he had ever encountered. Every shadow seemed to pulse with hidden danger, and the sense of being watched grew stronger with each passing second.

Richards, though not having seen the creature himself, trusted Brad's instincts. His mind flashed back to Captain Delgado's warnings and the unsettling changes in the environment they had witnessed. He knew they were not alone in these waters, and caution was their best ally.

Breaking the surface, they gasped for air, their breaths ragged from the adrenaline coursing through their veins. The morning light felt stark and harsh after the dim, suffocating depths. Brad looked at Richards, his eyes wide with lingering fear.

"Did you see it?" he asked, his voice trembling as he removed his mask.

Richards shook his head, but his expression was serious. "No, but I believe you. We need to get these fossils back and reassess our approach. Whatever's down there, it's not something we want to confront unprepared."

They swam back to the shore, their senses on high alert. Every ripple in the water, every distant splash seemed to echo with the presence of the unseen creature. The sense of danger was ever-present, a reminder of the primal world they had dared to invade.

Upon reaching the safety of the shore, Brad and Richards shared a knowing glance. The lagoon concealed dangers beyond their wildest fears, and the creature lurking beneath its surface was the sentinel of ancient enigmas. They would need to proceed with extreme caution if they hoped to unravel the secrets buried in the depths without becoming just another terrifying legend of the Black Lagoon.

"What happened?" Sarah asked, assisting them in removing their SCUBA gear.

"All I can say is that it was enormous. It looked human but was covered in fish scales. Its hands were as large as basketballs, with claws… claws that could easily rip someone apart," Brad recounted.

Richards looked at Brad. "Unfortunately, I did not see anything."

"We need to leave now," Emily, visibly shaken, urged. "Alan, we have enough fossils to continue our research back at the lab where it's safe. This is becoming far too dangerous for us."

Alan, the expedition's leader and financier, shook his head firmly. "No, we can't leave now. This is the find of the century. The secrets of this lagoon could rewrite history. "We're staying until we uncover the truth," he declared with unwavering determination.

Emily's eyes widened in fear and frustration. "But Alan, it's too dangerous! We barely made it out alive."

Richards remained resolute. "I understand the risks, but the potential rewards are too great to walk away from. We'll take extra precautions, but we're not leaving."

Brad and Sarah exchanged worried glances, knowing that convincing Alan to abandon the expedition would be impossible. The allure of the lagoon's mysteries had ensnared him completely, and there was no turning back now. Alan's determination to uncover the secrets of the Black Lagoon overshadowed any concern for their safety, and they all felt the weight of the impending dangers.

"So, what do you suggest we do now?" Sarah asked, her voice tinged with anxiety. "We have no weapons other than the spearguns, and who knows if that will be enough to defend ourselves from whatever it is that Brad saw?"

Before Alan could respond, Captain Delgado chimed in, his voice steady and reassuring. "Excuse me, but we have several weapons onboard the River Queen," he said. On cue, Jose, the lead deckhand, went into the cabin of the boat and returned carrying two rifles.

"These should provide some additional protection," Captain Delgado continued. "But we need to be smart about how we proceed. The creature is not just dangerous; it's also protecting something. We must stay alert and work together if we are to survive and uncover the secrets of this lagoon."

Brad took one of the rifles from Jose, inspecting it with a sense of grim determination. "We need a plan," he said. "We can't just dive back in without knowing what we're up against. We need to study its behavior, find its weaknesses."

Alan stepped forward, his eyes gleaming with excitement and resolve. "We'll set up a perimeter around the lagoon and monitor its movements. We can use the River Queen as our base and launch small, controlled dives to gather more information. This is the find of the century, and we can't let fear stop us now."

The group nodded in agreement, the gravity of their situation sinking in. They were on the brink of a monumental discovery, but the cost of that knowledge could be their lives. With newfound resolve, they prepared to face the dangers of the Black Lagoon, knowing that their quest for truth had only just begun.

As evening approached, the campsite settled into an uneasy quiet. Emily was deeply engrossed in examining her fossils, while the others seemed lost in their own thoughts, grappling with the terrifying implications of the creature Brad had encountered. The shadows lengthened, and the tension in the air was palpable.

Sarah walked over to Brad and put her arm around him, offering a comforting presence. Alan, noticing the intimate gesture, couldn't hide the flash of jealousy that crossed his face.

"I really wish Alan wasn't so hardheaded and would call off this expedition," Sarah whispered to Brad. "We need to return with more manpower and weapons. We have no idea what we're dealing with. Even if it took him a month or two to equip a new expedition force, I don't think this thing is going anywhere."

"I agree," Brad said, gently caressing the back of Sarah's head. "But sadly, Alan has replaced science with the almighty dollar and the pursuit of fame. He's blinded by the potential discovery, not thinking about the risks we're taking."

Sarah sighed, glancing over at Alan, who was pacing near the edge of the campsite, muttering to himself. "It's just frustrating. We're all in danger, and he's so focused on the headlines and the glory that he's ignoring the real threats."

Brad nodded. "We need to be cautious. If he won't call it off, we have to take matters into our own hands to ensure our safety. We can't let his ambition put us all at risk."

As the night deepened, the group gathered around a small campfire, its flickering flames casting eerie shadows. The jungle creatures who come out at night made their presence known with their calls. Captain Delgado handed out the rifles, ensuring everyone knew how to handle them. "We stick together," he said firmly. "No one goes off alone. We set watches through the night and keep our eyes and ears open."

Alan finally joined them, his face a mask of determination. "We're on the brink of something monumental," he said, his voice filled with conviction. "I know it's dangerous, but the discoveries we make here could change everything we know about history and evolution. We can't let fear hold us back."

Emily looked up from her fossils, her expression troubled. "Alan, I understand the importance of this discovery, but we need to balance that with our safety. If something happens to any of us, this expedition will be for nothing."

Alan nodded reluctantly. "You're right. We need to be careful. But we also need to press on. Tomorrow, we'll start our exploration again, but we'll be more prepared. We'll set up a perimeter, use the River Queen as our base, and proceed with caution."

The group agreed, though the sense of foreboding lingered. They knew the lagoon held secrets that were not meant to be disturbed, and as they settled in for the night, each of them wondered if they would make it through to see the dawn.

CHAPTER 7

Sarah saw Brad near the dying campfire the next morning and joined him, letting Emily sleep in.

"Coffee?" Brad asked, lifting a coffee pot and mug.

"If you tell me you already made breakfast, I think I will propose to you," she replied with a flirtatious smile.

"Gee, now I wish I had, but sorry, only coffee. How did you sleep?"

"Not well. I couldn't shut off my brain, and Emily tossed in her sleep all night long."

"I don't think anyone other than Alan slept well," Brad said as he filled the mug for Sarah.

Sarah took a sip of the steaming coffee and settled down next to Brad. "So, what do you think this thing is?"

Brad stared into the flickering embers, collecting his thoughts. "The water is pretty murky the deeper you go, and my focus was on finding more fossils. The sunlight plays tricks on you by bouncing off the tree roots and weeds. The only reason I saw it was that it decided to change positions. I mean, who knows how long it was watching Alan and me. I think that when I moved a little closer to where Alan was, it moved to get a better vantage point. Its movement stirred up the debris in the water."

He paused, the memory of the encounter replaying vividly in his mind. "It was massive, Sarah. It had a vaguely human shape but was covered in scales, almost like a gigantic fish or some prehistoric creature. Its eyes were dark and unblinking, giving off an eerie, almost intelligent gleam. The hands…like I said earlier, they were the size of basketballs, with long, sharp claws that looked like they could tear through anything. It moved with a fluid grace, almost like it was part of the water itself."

Sarah shivered despite the warm morning air. "Do you think it's been down there for a long time?"

Brad nodded slowly. "I do. It felt ancient, like something that's been hidden away for centuries. It's not just an animal; it's a guardian of this place. And I think it's protecting something, maybe even more than what we've discovered so far."

Sarah gazed into Brad's eyes, seeing the mixture of fear and fascination that mirrored her own feelings.

"We have to be careful, Brad. Alan's ambition is clouding his judgment. We need to make sure we don't end up as another legend of the Black Lagoon."

Brad squeezed her hand reassuringly. "We will. We'll stick together and watch out for each other. We've come too far to turn back now, but we won't be reckless. We'll find a way to uncover the truth without falling prey to it."

As the morning light broke through the jungle canopy, the camp began to stir. Alan emerged from his tent, his determination evident, but Brad and Sarah shared a silent pact: they would proceed with caution, ever mindful of the ancient terror lurking beneath the waters of the Black Lagoon.

"Good morning," Alan said, casting a glance at Brad and Sarah before eyeing the makeshift table of the camp. "What, no breakfast?" he added with a tone of disappointment before turning towards the River Queen. "Hey, Delgado. Where's breakfast? I'm paying you enough!"

Captain Delgado stirred from the boat's cabin, rubbing his eyes. "I'm sorry, Senor. We will get right on it." He quickly turned to his two deckhands, Jose and Manuel, who immediately began gathering supplies from the boat. They scurried to transport the provisions to the camp, setting up a portable stove and unpacking ingredients with practiced efficiency.

Brad and Sarah exchanged a glance, the tension between them and Alan momentarily overshadowed by the mundane task of preparing a meal. The morning sun climbed higher, casting a warm glow over the camp as the aroma of sizzling bacon and fresh coffee filled the air.

Delgado supervised the preparation, ensuring everything was up to Alan's standards. Despite the hurried start, the deckhands worked with a quiet determination, their movements swift and precise. Within minutes, plates of scrambled eggs, bacon, and toast began to emerge, offering a semblance of normalcy in the midst of their perilous expedition.

As the team gathered around the table, Alan's demeanor softened slightly. "Thank you, Delgado," he said, taking a seat and grabbing a plate. "Let's eat quickly. We have a lot of work ahead of us today."

The group settled down to eat, the tension from earlier easing as they focused on their breakfast. Emily joined them, her eyes still bleary from sleep, and gratefully accepted a steaming cup of coffee from Brad.

"Today, we need to map out the deeper sections of the lagoon," Alan began, his voice taking on a commanding tone. "We'll need to be thorough and cautious. This creature is dangerous, but it's also an incredible discovery. I take a speargun and be the overwatch," he said, looking at Brad.

Sarah glanced at Brad, concern etched on her face and then turned to Alan. "Just remember, we need to prioritize safety. No more risks than necessary. I suppose you would be against me joining you?"

"Sorry, but no place for a woman. Brad will map out the area and I will focus on any appearance of the creature. I can't be worried about you," Alan replied, though his eyes betrayed his relentless ambition.

With breakfast concluded, the team began to prepare for the day's work. They double-checked their equipment, ensuring everything was in order, and reviewed their plan of action. The lagoon awaited them, its murky depths holding secrets that both fascinated and terrified them.

Sarah and Emily helped both Alan and Brad put on their tanks. As they moved towards the water's edge, Brad couldn't shake the feeling of unease that had settled over him. The creature's image remained vivid in his mind, a stark reminder of the dangers that lurked below. They both slowly entered the water leaving behind a trail of bubbles reaching the surface.

Captain Delgado had his men clean up from breakfast and return to the River Queen with him. As they worked, the camp buzzed with the sounds of clinking dishes and the rustling of supplies. Sarah, noticing Delgado's ever-present cigar, couldn't resist a playful jab.

"Captain Delgado, do you ever light those cigars?" she asked with a mischievous smile.

Delgado laughed heartily and turned to Sarah. "No, senorita. They last longer if I do not light them," he replied, giving her a wink before heading back to the boat.

With the morning chores winding down, Emily and Sarah found themselves with a rare moment of quiet. They settled near the remnants of the campfire, the warmth of the fading embers a stark contrast to the chill of the morning air.

"So, Emily, tell me about yourself," Sarah began, her tone inviting and warm. "We've been working together for a while now, but I feel like I don't really know you."

Emily hesitated for a moment, then smiled softly. "Well, where to start? I grew up in a small town, always fascinated by the natural world. My parents were supportive but didn't really understand my passion for fossils and ancient history. They thought I'd outgrow it, but here I am."

Sarah nodded, encouraging her to continue. "What about your education? You're clearly brilliant."

Emily blushed slightly. "I studied paleontology and anthropology at Colorado State. Spent years digging through archives and going on small expeditions. This one, though, is the most intense and dangerous I've ever been on. And to be honest, it's making me jumpy. I've never been in a jungle this wild before, and the creature Brad saw... it's terrifying."

Sarah leaned in closer. "I get that. It's a lot to handle. But you're doing great. We all have our fears. I, for one, hate confined spaces. Always have."

Emily's eyes widened. "Really? I never would have guessed. You seem so composed."

Sarah chuckled. "Composed on the outside, maybe. But inside, I'm just as scared as everyone else. Especially now, with everything we're facing."

Emily sighed, her shoulders relaxing a bit. "It helps to know I'm not alone in feeling this way. My jumpiness... it comes from a bad experience during an expedition in the Amazon. We were ambushed by wildlife smugglers. I got out, but it left me a bit on edge."

Sarah reached out and squeezed Emily's hand. "That sounds awful. No wonder you're on high alert. But you're strong, Emily. We all are. We just need to stick together and support each other."

Emily smiled gratefully. "Thanks, Sarah. It means a lot. What about you? What brought you here?"

Sarah took a deep breath. "I guess I've always been a bit of an adventurer. Studied marine biology and archaeology, always chasing the next big discovery. But it's not just the science for me. It's the thrill, the unknown. And, I suppose, a bit of wanting to prove myself. My dad used to call me a female version of Indiana Jones."

Emily nodded. "I understand that. There's something about uncovering the past that's incredibly compelling. And here, in the Black Lagoon, we're on the brink of something extraordinary."

CHAPTER 7

The two women sat in comfortable silence for a moment, the bond between them growing stronger. The jungle around them felt a little less intimidating, the shadows a bit less menacing.

"I couldn't help but notice that you and Brad are very close," Emily ventured, curiosity in her eyes.

Sarah smiled softly. "Yes, it's not a secret that Brad and I love each other. Someday, we both want to get married."

"So, what's holding you back?" Emily asked, her tone gentle and understanding.

Sarah took a deep breath before answering. "I guess we're both too practical. I mean, we're fortunate to be on this expedition together, but since he and I have been a couple, many times we find ourselves on opposite sides of the world. For now, it hasn't hurt our relationship, but can a marriage hold up to long-distance partings?"

Emily nodded thoughtfully. "That's a tough situation. Long-distance is hard on any relationship. But it sounds like you two have a strong bond. Maybe you just need to find a way to balance your careers and your personal lives."

Sarah looked down, her fingers tracing patterns in the dirt. "It's just… we're both so passionate about our work. And our work often takes us to different places. We've talked about it, and we both want to make it work, but the uncertainty is always there."

Emily reached out and placed a reassuring hand on Sarah's arm. "I understand. My last relationship ended because he couldn't handle the travel and the unpredictability of my work. It's hard to find someone who understands and supports that part of you."

Sarah looked up, meeting Emily's eyes. "How did you cope with it?"

Emily shrugged. "It wasn't easy. I threw myself into my work, which helped, but it also made me realize how important it is to find someone who shares that same passion and can be flexible. It sounds like you and Brad have that, at least."

Sarah nodded, feeling a bit more hopeful. "Yeah, we do. And I think, deep down, we both know that we'll find a way. It's just the logistics that are tricky."

Emily smiled. "Well, if anyone can figure it out, it's you two. And hey, maybe this expedition will give you both the chance to really think about what you want for the future."

Sarah smiled back, grateful for the support. "Thanks, Emily. That means a lot."

As the morning light grew stronger and the camp came to life, Sarah and Emily stood up, ready to face the challenges of the day. Their conversation had brought them closer, and the friendship they were building felt like a new source of strength.

Both women jumped when they noticed movement in the water. Captain Delgado, ever vigilant, saw it too. Without hesitation, he grabbed a rifle, his eyes fixed on the spot, waiting for whatever might emerge. Just then, Brad and Alan surfaced, slowly making their way to the shoreline, their gear glistening with the water's shimmer.

Emily and Sarah hurried to their location, helping them remove their SCUBA gear. The air was filled with the sounds of their heavy breathing and the distant calls of the jungle.

"No sign of the creature?" Sarah asked, her voice tense with anticipation.

"No," Brad replied, shaking his head. He pointed to an area across from the River Queen. "We mapped out that whole section over there. Most of the fossils we've collected are heavily concentrated on this side of the lagoon. The other side is just a jumble of tree roots, plants, and fallen debris in various stages of decay."

"So, it was a waste of time?" Emily asked, her eyes fixed on Alan.

Alan frowned slightly, then his face brightened with excitement. "I won't say that. When we went to the area where Brad saw the creature yesterday, I found this on a rock." He held up a large fish scale, its surface glistening in the morning light.

Emily's eyes widened as she ran up to Alan, her fingers trembling slightly as she examined the scale. "My God. I have never seen a fish scale this size." She looked up at Alan, her curiosity palpable. "Can I put it under the microscope?" she pleaded, her voice filled with awe.

Alan nodded, handing the scale to Emily with careful hands. "Go ahead, but please don't damage it. That is our proof that there is something down there, and we are going to trap it."

Emily eagerly took the scale and rushed to the camp's makeshift laboratory. The team watched her disappear into the tent, the weight of their discovery hanging in the air. Sarah looked at Brad, her eyes reflecting the same mixture of excitement and fear that he felt.

"Do you think it's really that significant?" Sarah asked, her voice barely above a whisper.

Brad shrugged, his gaze fixed on the spot where the scale had been found. "I don't know, but it's something. If it's not a fish, then what is it? We need to understand its origin and its connection to the fossils we've been finding."

Alan joined them, his face alight with the thrill of discovery. "This could be our breakthrough. If we can find more evidence like this, we might just be able to prove that this creature is not just a myth but a living relic from a time long past."

Just then, Emily returned, her face glowing with excitement. "You have to see this," she said, her voice trembling with exhilaration. "The scale has patterns unlike anything we've seen before. It's almost like it's from a different era, a different species entirely."

She placed the scale under the microscope, and the group gathered around, their eyes wide with amazement. The intricate patterns on the scale were unlike anything they had studied before, each ridge and groove telling a story of ancient times.

"This is incredible," Brad murmured, his voice filled with wonder. "It's like we've stepped into a different world. Whatever this creature is, it's connected to the very fabric of the lagoon's history."

Alan nodded, his eyes reflecting the same awe. "We need to gather more evidence. This could be the key to understanding the lagoon's mysteries and proving that the creature is real. Let's set up traps, survey the area more thoroughly, and document everything we find. We're not just exploring anymore—we're uncovering history."

CHAPTER 8

As noon arrived, the heat and humidity became stifling, turning the jungle into a sweltering furnace. Alan and Brad, their shirts soaked through with sweat, decided to remove them, revealing chests glistening with perspiration. The oppressive heat showed no mercy, and their bodies quickly shimmered under the relentless sun.

Emily and Sarah, equally struggling with the soaring temperatures, retreated to the shade of their tents to change. Emerging moments later, they had swapped their previous attire for shorts and sleeveless tank tops, hoping the lighter clothing would offer some respite. However, the humid air clung to their skin, and their new outfits soon absorbed the ever-present perspiration.

The team continued their work, but the intense heat made every task feel arduous. The air was thick, each breath a reminder of the tropical environment that surrounded them. Even the simplest movements left them drenched in sweat, their clothes sticking uncomfortably to their bodies.

"God, it's like a sauna out here," Sarah muttered, wiping her forehead with the back of her hand. She glanced at Emily, who was fanning herself with a makeshift fan made from a large leaf.

"I don't think I've ever experienced heat like this," Emily replied, her voice strained. "It's exhausting."

Brad looked over at the women, concern etched on his face. "We need to stay hydrated. Let's take frequent breaks and make sure we're drinking enough water."

Alan nodded in agreement, his determination undeterred by the oppressive conditions. "We can't let the heat slow us down too much. We have a lot of ground to cover and not much time to do it."

Despite the grueling environment, the team pressed on, driven by their shared goal. They took turns retreating to the shade for brief respites, gulping down water and catching their breath before returning to their tasks. The camaraderie among them grew as they shared in the struggle, their mutual support helping them endure the harsh conditions.

During one of their breaks, Sarah and Emily found a moment to talk. "How are you holding up?" Sarah asked, handing Emily a canteen.

Emily took a long drink before answering. "It's tough, but I'll manage. We've come too far to let a little heat stop us now."

Sarah smiled, appreciating Emily's resolve. "That's the spirit. We just have to pace ourselves and keep an eye on each other. We're all in this together."

As the afternoon wore on, the team's persistence began to pay off. They meticulously documented their findings, each new discovery fueling their determination to uncover the lagoon's secrets. The heat continued to beat down on them, but their collective resolve remained unbroken.

By the time the sun began its descent, casting long shadows across the jungle, the team had made significant progress. They gathered around the campfire once more, sharing stories of the day's challenges and triumphs. The camaraderie they had built in the face of adversity gave them strength, a reminder that they were not just colleagues, but a team united by a common purpose.

The oppressive heat of the day had tested their limits, but it had also forged a stronger bond among them. As night fell, they knew that whatever lay ahead, they would face it together, ready to tackle the mysteries of the Black Lagoon with unwavering determination.

Captain Delgado, noticing the team struggling with the rising temperature, called out to Richards. "Mr. Richards, I recommend that you and your team take a siesta, like we do. Allow your bodies to rest. I promise you'll all feel much better after a nap."

"I'll take that under advisement, Captain," Alan replied. He turned to his team. "What do you all think?"

Everyone agreed and returned to their tents. Emily quickly fell asleep, sweat trickling down her forehead onto her pillow. Sarah tried to rest, but the tent only seemed to amplify the stifling heat. Feeling restless, she decided to seek relief.

While everyone else slept, Sarah quietly slipped out of her tent and walked to the river's edge. The cool water beckoned, and she slowly waded in, sighing with relief as the refreshing sensation enveloped her. She moved further into the river, the water soothing her overheated skin.

Unbeknownst to her, in the shadows of the river vegetation, the creature watched with fascination. Its dark eyes followed her every move, intrigued by the human who had dared to enter its domain.

Sarah continued to enjoy her swim, relishing the cool water that provided a much-needed respite from the oppressive heat. She floated lazily on her back, letting the gentle current carry her along. The tranquility of the moment was soothing, and for a brief time, she forgot the dangers that lurked within the depths of the lagoon.

Unbeknownst to Sarah, the creature beneath the water had been observing her with growing curiosity.

Drawn by her movements, it decided to mimic her, swimming directly underneath her. Its powerful body moved silently through the water, perfectly mirroring her every stroke and glide.

Sarah was blissfully unaware of the creature's presence, her mind drifting in the peacefulness of the lagoon. Suddenly, she felt something brush against her leg. She froze, her heart pounding in her chest. She tried to dismiss it as a piece of drifting vegetation or a passing fish. But when she felt the touch again, more deliberate and firm, she knew it was neither a root nor a vine.

Panic surged through her, and she let out a terrified scream. She began swimming frantically back to the shore, her strokes desperate and uneven. The water seemed to resist her, dragging her back toward the depths she was trying to escape.

Alan, alerted by her scream, grabbed a spear gun and rushed to the river's edge. His eyes scanned the water, searching for any sign of the threat. He spotted a dark shape just below the surface, its outline menacing and unmistakable. Without hesitation, he aimed the spear gun and fired.

The spear struck the creature in the shoulder, and it surfaced with a hideous scream that echoed through the jungle. Its eyes were filled with a mix of pain and fury as it thrashed in the water. Sarah, now almost at the shore, turned to see the creature's monstrous form before it disappeared back beneath the surface.

Brad rushed to Sarah's side, helping her out of the water. She was trembling, her eyes wide with fear and shock. "Are you okay?" he asked, his voice urgent and concerned.

She nodded, still catching her breath. "It touched me, Brad. It was right there, under the water."

"We need to stay alert," Alan said, his gaze fixed on the rippling water where the creature had vanished. "It's not going to let us explore its territory without a fight. Brad, we need to go back out and see if the creature is dead. We can then pull it to shore."

CHAPTER 9

After a long and fruitless search, Alan and Brad returned to the shoreline, frustration evident in their expressions. Captain Delgado and his team stood vigilantly, their eyes scanning the surface of the lagoon, rifles at the ready. The atmosphere was tense, each man prepared for the creature to reappear at any moment.

Determined not to give up, Alan and Brad donned fresh SCUBA gear once more. This time, they were both armed with spearguns, ready for any confrontation that might arise underwater.

"That last time I saw him after hitting him with the spear, he was heading in that direction," Alan said, pointing towards a distant part of the lagoon. Brad nodded, his face set with determination.

With a final check of their equipment, the two men submerged, stroking away from the shoreline. The water was murky, and visibility was low, but they moved with purpose, driven by the need to find the creature and uncover the secrets it guarded.

This area of the lagoon felt different from the others they had explored. The water here was darker, and the vegetation seemed denser and more foreboding. As Brad and Alan swam deeper, Brad motioned for Alan to look at the walls of the adjacent bank, which seemed distinct from the other areas they had searched.

The walls were covered with unusual rock formations and layers of soil that hinted at something ancient and untouched. Intrigued, Alan handed his speargun to Brad and pulled out his knife. Carefully, he began to dig into the rocks and soil, each scrape revealing more of the hidden structure beneath.

The soil was dense and compact, suggesting it had been undisturbed for centuries. Alan's knife unearthed fragments of what appeared to be ancient artifacts, pieces of stone tools, and bones embedded within the layers. His excitement grew with each discovery, his mind racing with the potential significance of these findings.

Brad kept a vigilant watch, the speargun ready, his eyes scanning the murky waters for any sign of movement. The eerie silence was only broken by the occasional clink of Alan's knife against the rocks. As Alan worked, he carefully collected samples, placing them into a waterproof bag to bring back for analysis.

"This is incredible," Alan thought, his excitement barely contained. "These could be the remnants of an ancient civilization, perhaps even evidence of early human activity in this region."

Brad glanced over at Alan, who was absorbed in his task. "Find something interesting?" he asked, his voice slightly muffled by the water.

Alan nodded, his eyes gleaming with enthusiasm. "More than interesting. This could change everything we know about this area. We need to analyze these samples as soon as we get back to camp."

Suddenly, a shadow passed overhead, and both men froze. The water around them seemed to grow colder, and the sense of foreboding returned with full force. Brad tightened his grip on the speargun, ready for whatever might come next.

The creature was near, they could feel it. But now, they had something tangible, something that could help them understand the secrets of the lagoon and perhaps even the creature itself. As they cautiously made their way back to the surface, the weight of their discoveries pressed upon them, mingling with the ever-present danger lurking beneath the waters.

With Alan's bag of samples secured, they began their ascent, eager to return to the relative safety of the shoreline. They knew that the next steps would be critical—analyzing the artifacts, understanding their implications, and preparing for the inevitable confrontation with the guardian of the lagoon.

Sarah and Emily ran to the shoreline to help Brad and Alan get out of the river. Emily saw the heavy-laden bag held by Alan. "Those look different than any of the other rocks and fossils we have found."

"The whole area over there is strikingly different than any part of the lagoon," Alan replies pointing to the direction where the samples were taken. As the four continued to admire the latest find, and walk back to the microscope on the table, Captain Delgado and his deckhands continued with their siesta.

On the starboard side of the boat, bubbles began to rise, slowly at first, but then more numerous. Gradually, the head of the creature emerged, its gills flapping as it transitioned from its watery environment to that of the land. With a deliberate motion, it placed a massive, webbed hand on the side of the boat and hoisted its eight-foot-tall frame over the edge. Its eerie eyes scanned the surroundings, listening for any sound but hearing none.

The creature started to move, its webbed feet striking a bucket and sending it clattering across the deck. The noise shattered the silence, and Jose, hearing the commotion, woke and walked to that side of the boat. As he turned the corner, he came face to face with the monstrous creature, which let out a blood-curdling roar.

"The River Devil! The River Devil!" Jose screamed in terror. Before he could react further, the creature slashed across Jose's chest with its razor-sharp claws, tearing through flesh and bone with horrifying ease. Jose's chest split open, his internal organs spilling out in a grotesque display. Blood gushed from the wound and poured from his mouth as he looked down in shock at the gruesome sight of his exposed chest before collapsing onto the deck.

The deck was quickly stained with Jose's blood, a crimson pool spreading out beneath his lifeless body. The creature stood over him, its gills flaring and nostrils twitching as it savored the scent of blood. The metallic tang filled the air, mingling with the stench of death. The sound of the creature's heavy breathing and the dripping of blood were the only noises breaking the silence of the night.

As the horrifying scene unfolded, the other crew members, alerted by Jose's scream, rushed to the deck. Their eyes widened in horror at the sight of the creature standing over Jose's mutilated body. Panic set in, and chaos erupted as they scrambled for weapons, desperate to defend themselves against the monstrous intruder.

The creature, sensing the growing commotion, let out another terrifying scream, its eyes gleaming with malevolent intelligence. It knew it had the advantage, and it relished the fear it had instilled in its prey. The confrontation was far from over, and the night had only just begun to reveal the horrors that awaited them. He then dove into the dark water.

"Delgado, what's going on over there?" Alan called out, shading his eyes from the setting sun's rays.

"It's the creature. It killed Jose. Dios mío, the River Devil is real. I saw it with my own two eyes," Delgado replied, his voice shaking with fear and disbelief.

"We're coming over. Don't touch anything," Alan yelled, his voice carrying across the river. Leaving Emily and Sarah behind, Alan and Brad quickly rowed from the camp to the River Queen. The urgency of their movements mirrored the anxiety that gripped them.

As they reached the boat, the second deckhand and Captain Delgado pointed to the other side where Jose's body lay. The deck was a gruesome scene, covered with his remains and a pool of blood. Among the carnage, the imprints of webbed feet could be clearly seen, a stark reminder of the creature's presence.

"Where did you last see it?" Alan asked Delgado, his voice strained with a mix of anger and fear.

"After it jumped into the river, it swam over there," Delgado replied, pointing to the direction where he and Brad had surveyed earlier that day.

"Could you tell if it was hurt? I hit it with a spear earlier," Alan inquired, his mind racing with the possibilities.

"No, Señor. If you hit it, it did not seem to slow it down," Delgado responded, shaking his head.

Alan and Brad exchanged a grim look, understanding the implications. The creature was not only real but also resilient and deadly. They knew they had to act fast before it could strike again.

Brad examined the scene more closely, noting the sheer violence of the attack. "This thing is strong and smart. It knew exactly where to strike."

Alan nodded, his determination hardening. "We need to track it and find its lair. It's not just about protecting ourselves now; we need to understand what we're dealing with."

Delgado, still visibly shaken, added, "Miguel and I are on high alert. We can't afford to lose anyone else."

Alan turned to Brad. "Let's get back to camp and regroup. We need to come up with a plan to capture or kill this thing before it takes another life."

Brad nodded in agreement. "We'll need all the gear we can muster. This creature won't go down easily."

As they rowed back to the camp, the weight of their mission pressed heavily on them. The creature's attack had escalated the situation from a mere expedition to a fight for survival. The team would need to combine their knowledge, resources, and courage to face the terror that lurked in the Black Lagoon.

Upon reaching the camp, Alan briefed Emily and Sarah on what they had seen. The shock was evident on their faces, but it was quickly replaced by a steely resolve.

CHAPTER 10

Delgado and Miguel, leaving the River Queen, joined the others at the camp table. The group sat in stunned silence, still reeling from the brutal attack. Alan finally broke the silence, his voice heavy with the weight of the situation. "Obviously, we are dealing with a creature that has no qualms about killing. To attack a defenseless man like Jose in such a vicious way…" He trailed off, unable to finish the thought. The horror of the attack hung heavily in the air.

Emily, her eyes blazing with anger and fear, turned to Alan. "What about now, Alan? Are you satisfied with the loss of a human being? Can we not get the hell out of here?" she demanded, her voice trembling with emotion.

Alan met her gaze, his expression resolute but troubled. “Emily, I understand your fear and anger. Believe me, I do. But leaving now won’t change what happened to Jose. We need to understand this creature, find a way to stop it, and if possible capture it, so no one else suffers the same fate.”

Sarah, her face pale but determined, added, “We have to finish what we started. We can’t let this creature continue to terrorize us. We need to find its lair and put an end to this.”

Delgado nodded, his voice steady despite the fear in his eyes. “We are in this together. We need to be smart and cautious, but we can’t run away. We owe it to Jose to see this through.”

Brad, silent until now, spoke up. “We need a plan. We need to be prepared for anything. This creature is dangerous and cunning. But we’re a team, and together, we can find a way to defeat it.”

The group, though shaken, felt a renewed sense of determination. They knew the road ahead would be fraught with danger, but they were united in their purpose. They would face the creature head-on, armed with their knowledge and their courage, and they would not rest until the river was free from its reign of terror.

No one spoke for a long time, the weight of the situation pressing down on them like the humid jungle air. Finally, Brad broke the silence, his voice thoughtful and measured. “I’ve been thinking. When

Alan and I went over to that side of the lagoon, it felt like we were entering an entirely new section of the river. The fauna changed, the rock formations and fossils were completely different."

Alan, his patience wearing thin, snapped, "We've gone over that. So what?" His irritation was clear, but Brad remained unfazed. Instead of responding to Alan, he turned his gaze to Captain Delgado.

"Captain, what is on the other side of the hill?" Brad pointed to an area on the other side of the river from where they had been diving. Delgado's expression grew serious, and he glanced at Manuel, who seemed to understand the implication of the question. Fear flickered in Manuel's eyes.

"Señor Brad," Delgado began, his voice low and filled with a foreboding tone, "that area contains the Black Lagoon. It holds many terrible things, evil spirits. Many people have made the mistake of going there, and no one has ever come back."

A shiver ran down Sarah's spine. "Evil spirits? What do you mean?"

Delgado sighed deeply, gathering his thoughts. "The local legends speak of a place cursed by ancient rituals, where the spirits of the past guard their secrets jealously. The Black Lagoon is said to be the heart of these mysteries, a place where nature and the supernatural intertwine."

Mgiuel nodded, adding in a trembling voice, "I have heard stories since I was a child. Stories of people vanishing without a trace, strange lights, and sounds that chill the soul. The Black Lagoon is not just a place—it's a living entity, hungry for those who dare to uncover its secrets."

The group exchanged uneasy glances. The tales sounded like folklore, yet the terror in Manuel's eyes was real. Brad felt a chill settle over him, despite the heat. "We need to go there," he said, his voice resolute. "That's where we'll find answers."

Alan, though still skeptical, couldn't ignore the gravity of the situation. "If we're going, we need to be prepared. We've seen what this creature can do."

Sarah, her heart pounding, spoke up, "We need a solid plan. We can't just walk into this place blindly. We need to know what we're dealing with and how to protect ourselves."

Delgado nodded. "To get to the Black Lagoon, we must backtrack several miles. There is a small tributary that breaks of from this channel. It is very narrow and we will only get so far. The rest of your travel will be on foot I'm afraid."

The night grew darker, the jungle around them eerily silent as if it too was holding its breath. The team felt the full weight of their decision. They would face the Black Lagoon, armed with courage and the hope of uncovering the truth behind the legends and the deadly creature that guarded them.

As they prepared their gear and readied themselves for the journey ahead, a palpable tension filled the air.

They were about to venture into the unknown, where the line between reality and nightmare blurred, and every step could be their last. The suspense of what awaited them was almost unbearable, but they knew there was no turning back now.

"Well, what are you waiting for, Captain? Turn the damn boat around," Alan demanded, his impatience clear.

Delgado, visibly irritated, took out his cigar and glared at Alan. "Señor, you may be the captain of your expeditionary crew, but on the River Queen, I give the orders. It would be foolish to set out at night in this channel and even more foolish to navigate once we find the Black Lagoon tributary. Now, I suggest you break camp and plan to sleep here on the River Queen. I will set out once the sun starts its climb."

Alan bristled at the reprimand but knew Delgado was right. The dangers of the river were amplified at night, and venturing into the Black Lagoon in darkness would be tantamount to suicide.

Brad, sensing the tension, stepped in. "Delgado's right. We need to be smart about this. Let's break camp and get some rest. We'll need all our strength for what's ahead."

Sarah and Emily nodded in agreement, already feeling the fatigue from the day's events. They began gathering their gear, the atmosphere heavy with unspoken fears and anticipation. The idea of sleeping on the River Queen, so close to where Jose had been brutally killed, was unsettling, but they had little choice.

As they settled onto the boat, Delgado and Miguel worked efficiently, securing the vessel and preparing it for the night. The stillness of the river was punctuated by the occasional call of nocturnal creatures, adding to the eerie ambiance.

Sarah, unable to sleep, found herself staring at the dark water, her mind racing with thoughts of the creature and the legends surrounding the Black Lagoon. Emily joined her, and they sat in silence for a moment, drawing comfort from each other's presence.

"What do you think we'll find there?" Sarah finally whispered.

Emily shook her head. "I don't know, but whatever it is, we need to be ready. This place... it's like nothing I've ever encountered before. It feels ancient, alive somehow."

Sarah nodded, feeling the same inexplicable connection to the land and water around them. "We'll face it together. Whatever happens, we'll figure it out."

As the first light of dawn began to pierce the horizon, Delgado and Miguel readied the boat for departure. The team, though weary, felt a renewed sense of purpose. The Black Lagoon awaited, with its secrets and dangers, and they were determined to uncover the truth.

The River Queen's engine rumbled to life, and Delgado expertly navigated the treacherous waters.

The journey to the Black Lagoon had begun, the suspense and tension palpable as the boat cut through the river's surface, each passing moment bringing them closer to the unknown.

As they approached the ominous tributary leading to the Black Lagoon, the air seemed to grow heavier, charged with an ancient energy. The team prepared themselves for whatever lay ahead, their resolve unbroken despite the fear that gnawed at their hearts. They were about to enter the heart of the mystery, and there was no turning back.

CHAPTER 11

As everyone watched Captain Delgado expertly guide the boat through the narrow channels, the tension of their journey was palpable. The dense foliage on either side seemed to close in on them, casting long shadows over the water. Emily, breaking the silence, decided it was the right moment to share her findings.

"I've analyzed the material Alan and Brad brought back before the creature's attack," she announced. "The rocks and fossils, including some of the attached vegetation, date back to the Late Cretaceous Period, from 90 to 66 million years ago."

"That's outstanding," Alan said, his excitement barely contained. "Perhaps this creature is a descendant of some form of dinosaur from that period of time."

"Wait," Sarah interjected, her tone cautious yet firm. "I don't disagree with Emily's dating of the material as coming from the Cretaceous Period, but think about what you're saying, Alan. Let's say somehow, a T-Rex is inside the area of the Black Lagoon. How in the hell would a single dinosaur exist for this period of time? It's absolutely impossible."

Brad, who had been quietly listening, chimed in. "Sarah's right. The idea of a dinosaur surviving undetected for millions of years defies everything we know about evolution and extinction. There must be another explanation."

Emily nodded, her brow furrowed in thought. "Maybe it's not a direct descendant, but some form of creature that has adapted over time, isolated in this unique environment. The Black Lagoon could have created a micro-ecosystem that preserved ancient life forms in ways we don't fully understand."

Captain Delgado, still focused on navigating the treacherous waters, added, "The locals have always believed this place to be cursed. Maybe there's some truth to the legends. The Black Lagoon might hold secrets that science has yet to uncover."

Miguel, standing next to Delgado, spoke up, his voice tinged with fear. "The stories say that the Black Lagoon is a place where time stands still, where the past and present collide. Maybe that's why these creatures can exist here."

The boat continued its slow journey, the oppressive atmosphere weighing heavily on everyone. They were nearing the heart of the Black Lagoon, a place shrouded in mystery and danger. The implications of their findings were both thrilling and terrifying.

As they drew closer to their destination, the water around them grew darker, almost black, reflecting the ominous name of the lagoon. The sounds of the jungle faded, replaced by an eerie silence that seemed to seep into their bones.

Alan turned to the group, his face serious. "We need to be prepared for anything. If this creature is truly a remnant from the Cretaceous Period, we're dealing with something far beyond our understanding. We have to approach this with caution and respect."

Brad nodded, gripping his speargun tighter. "Agreed. Let's not take any unnecessary risks. We need to document everything and gather as much evidence as possible."

Sarah and Emily exchanged a glance, their initial skepticism giving way to a sense of awe and curiosity. They were on the brink of a monumental discovery, one that could rewrite the history of life on Earth.

The River Queen finally came to a stop at the edge of the Black Lagoon. The air was thick with anticipation and the lingering scent of decay. The team readied their equipment, each person steeling themselves for what lay ahead.

As they prepared to disembark, the water around the boat rippled, a subtle reminder of the creature that lurked beneath the surface. Their journey into the unknown had begun, and there was no turning back now. The Black Lagoon awaited, with its secrets and its dangers, ready to reveal the mysteries it had guarded for millennia.

"There is something else we have not considered," Brad said thoughtfully. "Maybe that's why these creatures can exist here." He paused, allowing the weight of his words to sink in. "Perhaps we are not just dealing with one gillman, or whatever we decide to call the creature. Maybe there is a group or family of them."

Everyone fell silent as they absorbed this new possibility. The implications were staggering. If Brad was right, they weren't just facing a solitary anomaly, but an entire ecosystem hidden within the lagoon.

Alan broke the silence, his brow furrowed in concern. "A group of these creatures would explain the varying sightings and the range of behaviors we've observed. It would mean they have a breeding population, a social structure, and possibly even territorial behaviors."

Sarah nodded. "We need to reconsider our approach. If there are multiple creatures, our safety protocols need to be significantly upgraded. We might also need to rethink our conservation strategies. We could be looking at an entirely new species, with all the scientific and ethical responsibilities that entails."

Emily added to the discussion. "And it's not just about the numbers. If there's a family of them, it means they've adapted to survive here, right under our noses. We need to understand their environment, their food sources, their interactions with each other."

"Agreed," Alan said. "Our next steps need to include a thorough survey of the lagoon, so we can gather as much data as we can without disturbing them too much. We might also be able to trap one of them and take it with us for further study."

Sarah's eyes narrowed as she turned to face Alan, her voice steady and matter-of-fact. "Alan, we are now on the creature or creatures' home base. Trying to capture one of them will easily result in other deaths, not just theirs but possibly ours as well. We should gather what we can and get out of here. You can return, armed to the teeth if you want, and risk your own life, but I won't be a part of it."

The tension in the air was palpable as the team considered the gravity of the situation. Emily, sensing the escalating disagreement, stepped in. "Sarah's right. This isn't just a scientific expedition anymore. It's a matter of survival, both for us and potentially for an undiscovered species."

Brad, usually the voice of reason, nodded in agreement. "We need to proceed with extreme caution. Any aggressive actions on our part could provoke a defensive response from the creatures. We're in their territory now."

Alan sighed, running a hand through his hair. "I understand the risks, but think of the scientific breakthrough. Capturing even one of these creatures could provide invaluable data."

Sarah's expression softened slightly, though her resolve remained firm. "I get it, Alan. I really do. But the potential cost is too high. We're not equipped to handle a confrontation, and we don't know enough about these creatures to predict their behavior."

Emily added, "Plus, the stress of captivity could harm the creature. Our best approach is to observe and document as much as we can without interference. We can learn a lot from their natural behavior."

Brad concluded, "Let's focus on non-invasive methods for now. We can use remote cameras, drones, and sonar mapping to get the data we need. If we determine it's safe and ethical to capture one later, we can plan a return expedition with the proper resources and backup."

Alan reluctantly nodded, acknowledging the consensus. "Alright, non-invasive it is. Let's start preparing the equipment and planning our survey routes. We'll proceed with caution and respect for their habitat."

CHAPTER 12

The dense jungle pressed in on all sides as the boat rounded the bend in the river coasting into a quiet spot. The vibrant sounds of the jungle—chirping birds, buzzing insects, rustling leaves—suddenly ceased, plunging the crew into an eerie silence. It was as if they had crossed an invisible threshold into another world, one that held its breath in anticipation. The atmosphere was heavy, almost tangible, like stepping into a lost world, a prehistoric landscape untouched by time.

"This is as far as I dare to go," announced Captain Delgado, his voice hushed as if he feared breaking the spell of silence. He guided his boat near a large overhanging tree, its gnarled branches casting twisted shadows on the water. "Miguel, secure us to this tree and drop the rear anchor."

Miguel moved quickly, tying the boat to the tree with practiced efficiency and letting the anchor slip silently into the murky depths. The tension among the crew was palpable, each person keenly aware of the unnatural stillness that surrounded them.

Captain Delgado turned to Alan and the rest of the team, who were anxiously waiting to climb overboard into the two rowboats bobbing beside them. "The Black Lagoon is just around that bend in the river," he said, his tone laden with foreboding. "You will know it when you see it."

Alan exchanged uneasy glances with Sarah and Brad, their earlier arguments momentarily forgotten in the face of the looming unknown. The crew climbed into the rowboats, their movements careful and quiet, the silence amplifying every splash and creak.

"You remember in the first Jurassic Park movie when Hammond welcomes everyone to Jurassic Park. Well, look at this place. Welcome to Jurassic Park," Alan said, not expecting a response.

As they rowed around the bend, the change in the environment was immediate and startling. The foliage grew denser, darker, as if the very light was being consumed by the jungle. Thick vines hung like serpents from the towering trees, and the water turned an inky black, reflecting the shadowy canopy above.

Suddenly, they were there. The Black Lagoon stretched out before them, an expanse of dark, still water shrouded in mist. It was an otherworldly place, simultaneously beautiful and terrifying. The air was thick with tension, and the feeling of being watched was almost overpowering.

The rowboats glided to a stop at the edge of the lagoon. Alan felt a chill run down his spine as he surveyed the scene. The silence was absolute, the stillness unnerving. It was as if the jungle itself was holding its breath, waiting.

"Stay alert," Alan whispered, his voice barely more than a breath. "We don't know what we're dealing with yet and I have this strange feeling we are being watched."

The team nodded, their faces etched with a mixture of awe and apprehension. They began setting up their equipment, every rustle and clink sounding unnaturally loud in the oppressive quiet. They were intruders in this primeval sanctuary, and they all felt it.

"I have an idea," Alan announced, a spark of excitement in his eyes. He turned to face Brad. "Do you remember when you saw the creature the first time and we lost it? It disappeared around what would now be that hill over there."

"Okay," Brad replied, still a bit puzzled by Alan's line of thinking. "Where are you going with this?"

"Follow my logic," Alan said, sensing Brad's confusion and eager to explain. "When we lost sight of the creature the first time, neither you nor I saw any foliage on the shoreline move, which means the creature did not leave the river. And after I shot it with the spear, it vanished again, but there was no sign of it running through the jungle."

Brad's eyes widened as he began to understand. "So, you're suggesting that there might be an underwater passage between the tributary where we were last night and the Black Lagoon?"

Alan's smile broadened, a triumphant gleam in his eyes. "Exactly. It's the only explanation that makes sense. The creature must be using an underwater tunnel to move between the different parts of the river system without being detected."

The team exchanged glances, the implications of Alan's theory sinking in. An underwater passage would explain the creature's seemingly magical ability to appear and disappear without a trace.

"We need to find that passage," Sarah said, her voice filled with determination. "It could be the key to understanding the creature's behavior and habitat."

Alan nodded in agreement. "And if we can locate it, we might be able to set up monitoring equipment to track the creature's movements more accurately."

"Let's get the sonar equipment ready," Sarah suggested. "If there's an underwater tunnel, the sonar will pick it up."

As the team prepared their gear, the atmosphere was charged with a mix of excitement and apprehension. The discovery of an underwater passage could be a game-changer, but it also meant venturing into the unknown, where the creature held the advantage.

They launched the rowboats again, the silence of the Black Lagoon pressing in around them. Alan and Brad led the way, their eyes scanning the murky water for any signs of the elusive tunnel. The sonar equipment beeped steadily, each sound echoing in the quiet lagoon like a heartbeat.

After what felt like an eternity, the sonar pinged loudly, signaling a significant finding. The team held their breath as they examined the readout. There, beneath the surface, was a dark, narrow tunnel leading away from the lagoon.

"We found it," Alan whispered, his voice barely audible over the hum of the equipment.

The team exchanged triumphant smiles, the thrill of discovery momentarily overshadowing their fear. They had uncovered a crucial piece of the puzzle, and with it, a glimmer of hope in their daunting quest to understand and possibly coexist with the mysterious creature of the Black Lagoon.

"Let's get back to the River Queen and grab our diving gear," Alan said. He looked up into the sky. "We only have a few hours of sunlight left. I would like to at least see the passageway and then, over dinner, we can discuss our plan of attack."

CHAPTER 13

Delgado instructed Miguell to accompany Brad and Alan so he could assist them getting in and out of the rowboat with their gear. Sarah and Emily remained on the boat with Captain Delgado. Miguel rowed towards the large wall of jungle that separated the two tributaries.

"Row over there, Miguel. You can drop anchor, and while you wait for us, you'll be in the shade," Alan instructed. With Miguel's help, the two divers prepared to enter the river.

"Please be careful, Señores. The River Devil is already upset with us," Miguel warned, his voice trembling slightly.

Brad and Alan nodded solemnly before diving into the river. They secured their masks and checked their air supplies, then descended into the pitch-black water. The world above disappeared as they entered the murky depths, their flashlights piercing the darkness in search of an entrance.

They swam through the underwater foliage, meticulously scanning every crevice. Just as they were about to give up, Brad motioned urgently for Alan to come to his position. Alan swam over, and Brad pushed back a thick curtain of vegetation, revealing a hidden underwater entrance.

Brad grabbed the speargun from Alan and cautiously began to enter the passageway. The narrow tunnel felt suffocating, the weight of the water pressing in from all sides. Halfway through, Brad noticed that his air bubbles only had to travel a short distance before reaching the surface. Using his thumb, he signaled for Alan to surface.

Upon breaking through the water's surface, they found themselves in a massive, echoing cave. The air was damp and cool, a stark contrast to the oppressive heat outside. They removed their masks and air hoses, taking a moment to catch their breath and adjust to their surroundings.

"This doesn't look like the creature's living quarters. Only a bunch of footprints," Brad observed, his voice reverberating off the cavern walls.

Alan nodded, his eyes scanning the dimly lit space. "Yes, it looks like it's just used to traverse the two tributaries. Wait. What is that over there?" He pointed to a shadowy section of the cave wall.

They cautiously approached the side wall, and their flashlights illuminated a startling sight: a webbed hand and arm protruding from the rock, its claws looking menacing even in its fossilized state.

Alan removed his dive knife and began chipping away at the surrounding dirt that encased the object. The work was painstaking, every scrape echoing ominously in the cave's silence. After several tense minutes, they managed to free the fossilized limb.

"This made the dive more than rewarding," a triumphant Alan said, admiring their find. The ancient relic was a tangible link to the creatures they were studying, a piece of the puzzle they hadn't expected to find.

Satisfied with their discovery, Alan and Brad replaced their masks and air hoses, preparing to retreat to the river with their precious find. As they descended back into the dark water, the enormity of their discovery weighed heavily on them. They knew this relic could be the key to unlocking the secrets of the Black Lagoon and its mysterious inhabitants.

***

Holding the clawed hand like a trophy, Alan emerged from the water and displayed the fossil to Captain Delgado, Sarah, and Emily. The ancient, webbed appendage looked both fragile and menacing, a relic from a time long past.

"Wow. What did you two find?" Sarah joked, her eyes wide with a mixture of awe and disbelief as she examined the clawed hand.

Alan grinned, his excitement on full display. "Apparently, in the past, these two sections of the river separated, and in the process, a creature was trapped. Kind of like being caught in an avalanche."

Emily leaned in closer, her scientific curiosity piqued. "So, you think there might be more of the specimen still trapped in the soil?"

Alan nodded. "It's possible. The conditions that preserved this part of the creature might have done the same for other parts. We'll go back tomorrow with a pick and see if there's more of the specimen still buried in the soil."

Captain Delgado, who had been watching silently, finally spoke. "This discovery could be incredibly significant. It proves that these creatures have been here for a very long time, no?"

Sarah added, "Yes, and it means there's a lot more we need to learn about their history and how they've survived here."

The team shared a moment of silent contemplation, the weight of their discovery settling in. They were uncovering the secrets of a lost world, one that had remained hidden beneath the waters of the Black Lagoon for millennia.

"We'll need to be careful," Brad said, breaking the silence. "This find is just the beginning. If there are more fossils, they could give us invaluable insights into the biology and evolution of these creatures."

Emily nodded in agreement. "And we'll need to document everything meticulously. This could change our understanding of the ecosystem here entirely."

As the group made plans for their next expedition, the sense of anticipation and excitement was palpable. They were on the brink of a major scientific breakthrough, one that promised to reveal the hidden history of the Black Lagoon and its mysterious inhabitants.

That evening, a festive mood enveloped everyone aboard the River Queen. Captain Delgado had rigged a makeshift BBQ at the stern of the vessel, and Miguel was busy grilling some freshly caught fish. The enticing aroma of the cooking fish mingled with the fresh river air, creating an atmosphere of celebration and camaraderie.

A loud pop echoed across the river as Alan opened a bottle of champagne, the sound breaking the tranquil evening. "I'd like to make a toast," he announced, his voice filled with pride and excitement. "Even if the fossil we found today is all we take back with us, we have made the greatest discovery of the 21st century."

He carefully poured champagne into paper cups, the bubbles dancing in the dim light of the setting sun. The team gathered around, their faces illuminated by the warm glow of the BBQ and the anticipation of their shared achievement.

Alan raised his cup, and everyone followed suit, their eyes reflecting the joy and sense of accomplishment that filled the air. "To discovery," Alan continued, his voice steady and filled with emotion. "To the hard work, dedication, and curiosity that brought us here. May this be just the beginning of many more incredible finds."

A chorus of "Cheers!" rang out as they clinked their paper cups together, the sound of their celebration blending with the gentle lapping of the river against the boat. The champagne flowed freely, and laughter echoed into the night as they recounted the day's adventures and speculated about what tomorrow might bring.

As they enjoyed the delicious grilled fish and shared stories under the starlit sky, a profound sense of unity and purpose settled over the group. They were not just colleagues on a scientific expedition; they were a team bound together by a shared dream and the thrill of exploration.

For a moment, the challenges and dangers of the Black Lagoon seemed far away, replaced by the warmth of friendship and the promise of new discoveries. The night wore on, filled with toasts and laughter, each person reveling in the triumph of their historic find.

CHAPTER 14

Feeling somewhat secure on the River Queen, everyone but Sarah and Brad decided to turn in early. Tomorrow would be filled with excitement and anticipation of finding more fossil remains of the creature. The others retired to their cabins, leaving the two of them alone on the deck under the blanket of stars.

Sarah leaned against the railing, gazing out over the dark water, lost in thought. Brad joined her, their shoulders brushing gently. The air was filled with the soft sounds of the night, a stark contrast to the earlier festive noise.

"It's been quite a day," Brad said softly, breaking the comfortable silence.

Sarah nodded, turning to face him. "It has. Today felt like we were part of something much bigger than ourselves."

Brad took a deep breath, his heart pounding. He had been waiting for the right moment, and now, under the vast expanse of the night sky, it felt perfect. "Sarah, there's something I've been meaning to ask you."

She looked at him, her eyes wide with curiosity and a hint of apprehension. "What is it, Brad?"

He took her hands in his, feeling the warmth and strength that had drawn him to her from the beginning. "Sarah, will you marry me? I know our lives are complicated, and we'll have to be apart sometimes, but I don't want to let that stand in the way. I love you, and I want to spend the rest of my life with you."

Tears welled up in Sarah's eyes, her heart swelling with emotion. "Oh, Brad," she whispered, her voice trembling. "Yes, yes, I'll marry you! I love you too, and we'll make it work, no matter what."

They embraced, the world around them fading away as they shared a passionate kiss. In that moment, surrounded by the serenity of the river and the promise of new discoveries, their hearts beat as one, united by love and the adventures that lay ahead.

The night wore on, filled with whispered promises and dreams of the future. As they finally parted to rest, they knew that whatever challenges they faced, they would face them together, bound by their love and the shared journey of discovery.

Miguel, feeling the effects of too much champagne, staggered out onto the deck of the River Queen. The festive mood had taken its toll, and his stomach churned uncomfortably. He leaned over the side of the boat, the cool night air providing little relief as he retched into the dark water below.

Unbeknownst to him, a pair of eyes watched from the shadows. The creature, hidden among the reeds on the shoreline, had been observing the evening's festivities with a cold, calculating gaze. It had seen Brad and Sarah retreat to their room and now, under the cover of night, it moved silently towards the boat.

The full moon cast a silvery glow over the river, illuminating the creature's path as it slipped into the water. Its powerful limbs propelled it swiftly and silently towards the River Queen, the ripples of its passage barely disturbing the surface.

Miguel, still hunched over the side, was oblivious to the approaching danger. His mind was focused solely on his discomfort, and he didn't hear the faint splashing sounds behind him as the creature emerged from the water and climbed onto the deck.

In a swift, fluid motion, the creature stood up, towering over the unsuspecting Miguel. It moved with lethal precision, its clawed hand swiping through the air. Miguel barely had time to gasp before the creature decapitated him with a single, brutal strike.

His lifeless body crumpled to the deck, blood pooling around it as his head tumbled into the river.

The creature paused, its dark eyes scanning the deck. The full moon provided enough light to navigate, and it moved silently, stalking the boat with an eerie grace. It crept along the shadows, its senses alert and ready, seeking out any remaining humans who might pose a threat or an opportunity.

Meanwhile, Brad and Sarah, oblivious to the horror unfolding outside, were lost in their newfound commitment to each other, planning their future together. The quiet of the night, now marred by a silent predator, seemed to hold its breath, waiting for the next moment of terror to unfold.

The creature continued its silent exploration of the River Queen, every muscle tense and ready. It was a master of its environment, and tonight, it had ventured into the heart of human territory, driven by instincts as ancient as the lagoon itself.

Captain Delgado, accustomed to the subtle sounds of the River Queen and the Amazon, was awakened by an unusual splash in the water. Instincts honed over years of navigating the river told him something was amiss. He started to leave his cabin but then quickly returned to grab his rifle and a flashlight.

As he stepped out into the dimly lit corridor, the air felt charged with an unspoken threat. He moved cautiously, his senses on high alert. As he approached the starboard side of the vessel, he sensed movement in the shadows. The beam of his flashlight cut through the darkness, revealing a sight that sent a chill down his spine: the headless body of Miguell sprawled on the deck, a pool of blood spreading beneath it. Standing over the corpse was the creature, its dark eyes gleaming with predatory intent.

The creature turned, its massive, clawed arms raising menacingly as it began to advance on Captain Delgado. Without hesitation, Delgado directed the flashlight beam at the creature's face. The sudden light elicited a guttural scream from the creature as it tried to shield its eyes from the blinding glare.

Seizing the moment, Delgado raised his rifle and fired, the shot echoing through the night. The bullet struck the creature's left arm, eliciting another agonized scream. Wounded, the creature leaped into the water with a splash, disappearing into the inky depths.

The commotion had awakened everyone else on the River Queen. They rushed to Delgado, their faces pale with fear and confusion. Emily screamed at the sight of Manuel's decapitated corpse and the blood-soaked deck.

"I hit it in the arm," Delgado announced, his voice steady despite the adrenaline coursing through him.

"Look, over here," Sarah yelled, pointing to a trail of blood mixed with iridescent scales leading away from the scene.

Regaining her composure, Emily took charge. "Someone gather the creature's blood and scales.

We need to analyze them." The team sprang into action, carefully collecting samples from the deck. The atmosphere was tense, a mix of horror and determination driving their actions. They knew that understanding more about the creature could be the key to their survival and the success of their mission.

As they worked, Delgado kept his rifle at the ready, his eyes scanning the dark water for any sign of the creature's return. The night, once filled with the promise of discovery, had turned into a harrowing fight for survival. But they were determined to face whatever dangers the Black Lagoon held, armed with newfound resolve and a growing understanding of the ancient predator that lurked in its depths.

CHAPTER 15

"Alan, I know you're tired of hearing me say it, but we now have two deaths committed by the creature," Emily said, her voice edged with determination and a hint of desperation. "You have the fossil remains of a creature's hand and tons of related material. Now is the time to leave this Godforsaken area and return to civilization."

Alan looked at Emily, seeing the exhaustion and fear in her eyes. The weight of their discoveries and the horrors they had witnessed pressed heavily on all of them. He knew she was right, yet the scientist in him hesitated, drawn to the potential for even greater discoveries.

"Emily, I understand how you feel," Alan began, his voice calm but strained. "We've lost Manuel and Jose, Captain Delgado's entire crew. This place has proven to be more dangerous than we anticipated. But think about what we've uncovered. We're on the brink of something monumental. Leaving now would mean abandoning a treasure trove of scientific knowledge."

Emily's eyes flashed with anger and concern. "Alan, what good is that knowledge if we're not alive to share it? We've already made incredible discoveries. The fossil hand alone is groundbreaking. We have more than enough to study and present to the world. But we need to be alive to do that."

She took a step closer, her voice softening but remaining firm. "I'm not just worried about our safety. I'm worried about you. I've seen the way you push yourself, how you're driven by the need to uncover every secret this place holds. But sometimes, we have to know when to stop. When to prioritize our lives over our work."

Alan sighed, running a hand through his hair. The logical part of him knew she was right, but the passionate scientist in him struggled to let go. "You're right, Emily," he finally admitted. "We've already paid a high price for our discoveries. It's time to regroup and return to safety."

Emily nodded, relief washing over her. "Thank you, Alan. We can come back with better preparation, more equipment, and a safer approach. For now, we need to get out of here and ensure we all make it back alive."

The rest of the team, overhearing the conversation, nodded in agreement. The decision to leave was unanimous, driven by the shared desire to survive and to honor the memories of those they had lost.

Alan walked into Captain Delgado's quarters, his face a mask of sorrow and determination. "I'm sorry, Captain, for your loss," he began, his voice heavy with empathy. "I don't know if you overheard, but my team wants to leave tomorrow for everyone's safety."

Captain Delgado looked up, his eyes filled with grief and anger. The loss of Miguel, his trusted crewmate, weighed heavily on him. "I understand their concerns, Senor Alan," he replied, his voice strained. "But we can't just abandon this mission after what happened."

Alan nodded, leaning in slightly as if to share a secret. "I feel the same way, Captain. We've lost good people, and I can't stand the thought of that creature getting away with it. We've made incredible discoveries, but there's still more out there. And we need to ensure that creature is no longer a threat."

Delgado's eyes narrowed, catching the subtle hint in Alan's words. "What are you suggesting?"

Alan lowered his voice, a conspiratorial tone creeping in. "What if we hunted the creature ourselves tonight, after everyone goes to bed? Just the two of us, and take care of this creature once and for all? We can tell the others it's for their safety. When they go to sleep, we'll take the rowboat to the passageway and capture or kill the creature."

The captain's expression hardened, a glint of resolve appearing in his eyes. "You're talking about revenge, Senor."

"Revenge and safety," Alan corrected. "We can't let this thing roam free, endangering anyone else. If we blind it with a powerful flashlight, hit it with a stun gun, and then wrap it in a heavy-duty net, we can capture it. We'll bring it back to the River Queen and secure it to the deck. At dawn, we'll set sail and be out of here."

Delgado considered the plan, the desire for justice and retribution burning in his chest. "Alright, Dr. Richards. We'll do it. For Miguel and for Jose."

As the night wore on, the rest of the team, feeling somewhat secure, decided to turn in early. The anticipation of leaving the dangerous lagoon brought a semblance of peace to the beleaguered crew. Alan and Delgado, however, remained awake, their minds focused on the task ahead.

When the boat was quiet, and the others were sound asleep, Alan and Delgado gathered their equipment and silently lowered a rowboat into the water. They rowed towards the passageway, the full moon casting an eerie glow on the water's surface, guiding their path.

Arriving at the passageway, they moved with stealth and precision. Alan held the powerful flashlight, ready to blind the creature, while Delgado gripped the stun gun. As they entered the passage, their nerves were taut, every sound amplified in the oppressive silence.

Suddenly, the creature appeared, its dark form emerging from the shadows. Alan quickly shone the flashlight into its eyes, causing the creature to scream and thrash, trying to shield itself from the blinding light. Delgado seized the moment, firing the stun gun and hitting the creature squarely.

The creature convulsed, momentarily incapacitated. Working quickly, they wrapped it in the heavy-duty net, securing the creature tightly. The triumphant feeling surged through them as they dragged the creature back to the rowboat and began the arduous journey back to the River Queen.

Upon their return, they alerted the entire crew. Everyone rushed to the deck, their eyes widening in disbelief and awe at the sight of the captured creature. With coordinated effort, they secured the creature to the deck, ensuring it was firmly restrained.

"We'll set sail at dawn," Alan announced, his voice filled with both relief and pride. "We've done it. We've captured the creature."

The team, though still shaken by the recent losses, found a renewed sense of purpose and hope. They had faced the dangers of the Black Lagoon and emerged victorious, ready to share their extraordinary discoveries with the world.

CHAPTER 16

Emily carefully prepared a syringe, her hands trembling slightly with a mixture of excitement and apprehension. She approached the restrained creature on the deck of the River Queen, its massive form writhing weakly in the heavy-duty net. The team watched intently, the air thick with anticipation.

"I've never done this before," Emily admitted, her voice steady despite her nerves. "I'm only guessing how much sedative to administer. We don't have any data on the creature's physiology, so I have to be cautious."

She inserted the needle into the creature's scaly arm and slowly depressed the plunger, administering the sedative. The creature's movements gradually slowed, its breathing becoming deep and rhythmic as it succumbed to the drug.

"That should hold it for the night," Emily said, stepping back and observing the creature closely. "I'll monitor its vital signs periodically to ensure it remains stable. I can't wait to get back to my cabin and analysis its blood."

The team nodded, relief mingling with the ever-present tension. As the night drew on, they made preparations to rest, knowing they needed their strength for the journey ahead.

Alan took the first watch, positioning himself near the restrained creature with his rifle close at hand. The deck was quiet, save for the gentle lapping of the river against the hull and the soft murmurs of the team settling down for the night.

Sarah approached Captain Delgado, who was leaning against the steering wheel of the boat, gazing out at the dark water. She joined him, the silence between them comfortable and filled with unspoken understanding.

"Captain," Sarah began, breaking the quiet, "I wanted to thank you for everything you've done. I know it hasn't been easy."

Delgado sighed, a wistful smile playing on his lips. "I've had my share of challenges, Sarah. This one's just... different." He paused, his eyes reflecting the moonlight. "I was once married, you know. No children."

Sarah looked at him, surprised by the revelation. "Really? What happened?"

He shrugged, a hint of sadness in his voice. "She accused me of being in love with the Amazon more than with her. In a way, she was right. This place has always held a piece of my heart, something I could never fully explain. We drifted apart, and eventually, she filed for divorce. With no kids it wasn't complicated."

Sarah nodded, understanding the complexities of love and passion. "It's hard to balance such a strong calling with personal relationships."

Delgado smiled softly. "Yes, it is. But I don't regret my choices. The Amazon has given me a sense of purpose, a connection to something greater than myself. And now, with everything we've discovered, I feel like it's all been leading to this moment."

They stood in silence for a while, each lost in their thoughts. The shared conversation had brought a sense of closeness, a bond forged in the trials and triumphs of their expedition.

As the night deepened, Sarah bid Delgado goodnight and retired to her quarters. Alan, still on watch, gave her a reassuring nod as she passed by. The River Queen was quiet, the team's resolve strengthened by their shared experiences and the promise of new discoveries.

The night wore on, filled with the quiet sounds of the river and the steady breathing of the sedated creature. Alan kept his vigil, his mind racing with thoughts of what lay ahead. They had captured the creature, but the journey was far from over. They would face whatever came next with determination and unity, ready to reveal the secrets of the Black Lagoon to the world.

Emily could not believe her eyes as she checked and rechecked her findings of the creature's blood. The data was astonishing and groundbreaking, confirming her earlier hypothesis. The creature was asexual and could reproduce on its own. This discovery threw a whole new hypothesis into their research and understanding of the creature's biology.

Excited and eager to share the news, she quickly left her cabin, hoping to run into anyone from the team. Her mind raced with the implications of this finding as she navigated the narrow corridors of the River Queen.

She found Alan on watch, his eyes scanning the dark water while he remained vigilant by the restrained creature. Approaching him, she could barely contain her excitement.

"Alan, you're not going to believe this," she said, her voice filled with a mixture of awe and urgency.

Alan turned to her, immediately sensing the importance of what she was about to say. "What is it, Emily?"

"I've rechecked the creature's blood samples multiple times. It's confirmed—this creature is asexual. It can reproduce on its own," she explained, her words tumbling out in a rush.

Alan's eyes widened in surprise. "That's incredible. It changes everything we thought we knew about these creatures. If it can reproduce without a mate, it could explain how they've managed to survive in isolation and why they're so territorial."

Emily nodded, her excitement barely contained. "Exactly. This discovery is monumental. We need to document everything thoroughly and consider the broader ecological impacts. But first, we need to get everyone to safety and out of this dangerous area."

Alan agreed, the revelation adding another layer of complexity to their mission. "We'll address this fully when we're back in a secure environment. For now, let's focus on getting through the night and leaving at dawn."

"What's all the excitement about?" Brad asked as he approached, with Sarah following close behind. "Is the creature secure?"

Emily nodded, her expression serious yet animated. "Yes, the creature is secure. I was just sharing with Alan what I found analyzing the creature's blood. It's asexual."

Brad's eyes widened in surprise. "What? That completely changes our understanding of it."

Sarah chimed in, equally astonished. "An asexual creature that can reproduce on its own... this will revolutionize our approach to studying its behavior and ecosystem."

Brad nodded, deep in thought. "We need to rethink everything we know about its survival and territorial instincts. This discovery could have major implications for our research."

As the night wore on, the rest of the team, feeling somewhat secure, decided to turn in early. The anticipation of leaving the dangerous lagoon brought a semblance of peace to the beleaguered crew. Alan remained on watch, positioning himself near the restrained creature with his rifle close at hand. The deck was quiet, save for the gentle lapping of the river against the hull and the soft murmurs of the team settling down for the night.

CHAPTER 17

Emily approached the restrained creature once more, her mind buzzing with the implications of their discovery. She wanted to gather a few more samples to ensure the validity of her findings. With Sarah by her side, she knelt beside the creature, her equipment in hand, she didn't notice the subtle shift in its breathing pattern.

Just as she was about to insert the syringe again, the creature's eyes snapped open. In a blur of motion, it twisted and snapped through the weakened net, its powerful tail lashing out and knocking Emily off her feet. The team sprang into action, but they were too late. The creature seized Sarah in its strong grip and dove over the side of the River Queen, disappearing into the dark waters below.

"Sarah!" Alan shouted, rushing to the edge of the boat, his rifle at the ready. The water churned violently where the creature had vanished, but there was no sign of Sarah or the creature.

Captain Delgado barked orders, his calm demeanor cracking under the sudden chaos. "We need to get her back. Alan, get the spotlight on the water. Emily, Brad, prepare the tranquilizers. We have to move fast!"

Panic and determination filled the air as the team scrambled to follow Delgado's commands. Alan swept the spotlight across the river's surface, desperately searching for any sign of Sarah or the creature. Emily and Brad loaded the tranquilizer darts, their hands shaking with a mix of fear and urgency.

"Over there!" Alan shouted, spotting a disturbance in the water. He aimed his rifle, ready to fire if necessary, while the others prepared to deploy the tranquilizers.

Sarah struggled against the creature's grip, her lungs burning as they plunged deeper into the cold, murky water. She knew she had to remain calm, conserve her energy. Her mind raced, searching for a way to break free or signal the team.

As the creature slowed, Sarah realized they were nearing the bottom of the lagoon. With a surge of determination, she managed to free one arm and reached for the small diving knife she always kept with her. She stabbed at the creature's arm, forcing it to loosen its grip slightly.

Above the surface, the team watched in tense silence as the water finally calmed. They had no idea if Sarah was alive or if the creature had taken her to its lair.

"We can't wait any longer," Delgado said, his voice filled with resolve. "We have to go in after her. Alan, Emily, Brad, you're with me. Captain, keep the boat ready and the spotlight on us. Let's move."

With that, they donned their diving gear and plunged into the water, following the trail of bubbles left by the creature. They descended into the depths, determined to rescue their friend and colleague, unaware of the dangers that awaited them below.

The team descended into the murky depths, their flashlights cutting through the darkness as they followed the trail of bubbles. The water grew colder and the pressure increased as they ventured deeper, but their determination to rescue Sarah kept them moving forward.

Suddenly, Alan's flashlight beam illuminated the entrance to a cave, its dark mouth beckoning ominously. He signaled to Brad, pointing towards the cave. He nodded in understanding and cautiously swam inside, the narrow passageway barely wide enough for them to navigate through.

Inside the cave, the water was eerily still, and their movements stirred up clouds of silt, making it difficult to see. They pressed on, their flashlights revealing the rough walls and jagged rocks surrounding them. The passageway twisted and turned, leading them further into the depths.

Eventually, the cave opened up into a larger chamber. Alan's heart sank as he realized there was no sign of Sarah. They scanned the area frantically, hoping for any clue that might lead them to her.

"We have to go back," Alan signaled, his eyes reflecting the same worry and determination. "We'll find another way."

Reluctantly, they retraced their path, emerging from the cave and heading back to the River Queen with the rowboat. Captain Delgado helps them aboard, his face filled with anxious anticipation.

" You didn't find her?" he asked, his voice trembling.

"No sign of her," Alan replied, stripping off his diving gear. "We found that cave that acts as a passageway to that other part of the river. We need to use the radar to find any other entrances nearby."

Delgado took command, instructing Brad to fire up the radar. The screen flickered to life, displaying the topography of the riverbed and surrounding areas. They scanned the map intently, looking for any anomalies that might indicate another cave entrance.

"There," Emily said, pointing to a spot on the screen. "That looks like it could be another entrance, not far from here."

"Let's move," Delgado ordered. "We don't have much time."

The River Queen's engine roared to life as they navigated towards the new location, the team's resolve unwavering despite the uncertainty. The spotlight swept the water's surface, guiding them to the potential entrance.

As they approached the designated spot, they saw a small, partially submerged opening in the rocky riverbank. It was barely visible in the dim light, but it was their best hope.

Alan and Brad quickly donned their diving gear once more, ready to explore the new cave. Delgado stayed on the boat, monitoring the radar and keeping the spotlight trained on the entrance.

"Be careful," he warned. "We don't know how many we might be dealing with in there." With a nod, Alan and Brad dove back into the water, swimming towards the cave entrance. They squeezed through the narrow opening, their flashlights cutting through the darkness as they ventured inside.

The passageway was tight and claustrophobic, but they pressed on, determined to find Sarah. After what felt like an eternity, the passage widened into another chamber. This time, their flashlights revealed a shocking sight.

Sarah was there, alive but unconscious, lying on a ledge above the water. The creature was nowhere to be seen. Alan and Brad quickly swam to her side, checking her vital signs. She was breathing, but weak and disoriented.

"Sarah, it's us," Brad said softly, shaking her gently. "We're here to take you back."

Sarah's eyes fluttered open, and she managed a weak smile. "I knew you'd come," she whispered.

Together, they carefully lifted her into the water, supporting her as they swam back through the passageway. Emerging from the cave, they signaled to Delgado, who helped them aboard the River Queen.

"Let's get her to the medical bay," Emily said, relief flooding her voice. "We need to get her stabilized and then figure out our next move."

As they tended to Sarah, the team couldn't help but feel a renewed sense of hope. They had found her, and now they had to prepare for whatever lay ahead. The Black Lagoon still held many secrets, and they were determined to uncover them all, no matter the cost.

Suddenly, the boat rocked violently, causing everyone to stumble. Captain Delgado, ever vigilant, felt the movement and grabbed his rifle. His eyes scanned the dark water, then widened in alarm as he saw the creature's massive form emerging from the depths, climbing onto the River Queen.

"It's back!" he shouted, his voice cutting through the night.

Brad, who was helping Sarah and Emily, immediately left their side and grabbed his rifle. The creature's eyes glowed with rage as it advanced towards them, water dripping from its scaly body. Its roar echoed across the deck, sending chills down their spines.

"Get ready!" Delgado shouted, positioning himself to face the advancing beast.

Brad and Alan joined him, all three aiming their rifles at the creature. As it lunged towards them, they opened fire, the deafening sound of gunshots filling the air. Bullet after bullet tore into the creature's tough hide, but it continued its relentless advance, driven by fury and pain.

The creature let out a violent roar, its body convulsing as the bullets tore through it. Blood sprayed across the deck as it finally stumbled, its strength waning. With a final, anguished cry, it fell over the side of the River Queen and plunged back into the river.

The team watched in tense silence as the water churned where the creature had fallen. Bubbles trailed back towards the cave where they had found Sarah, but then, abruptly, the bubbles stopped.

"Did we get it?" Brad asked, his voice barely above a whisper.

Delgado and Alan lowered their rifles, their breathing heavy with adrenaline.

"I don't know," Delgado replied, his eyes fixed on the now still water. "But we can't take any chances. We need to get out of here and report this."

"No," Alan said emphatically. "We have to make sure the creature is dead. We can't let it terrorize someone else in the future. Plus, if it is dead, we can tow its remains back to the River Queen and take it back to the mainland."

"I don't know, Alan," Brad said. "Sarah has several lacerations and needs to be treated."

CHAPTER 18

Alan went into the cabin where Emily was still treating Sarah. "Emily, how is she doing?" he asked.

"She's stable. None of her wounds are serious. Mostly scratches. My primary concern is infection, but I have administered several injections of antibiotics. She should be fine."

Alan turned to Brad. "We need to find the creature and confirm it is dead."

"Alright, Alan. But if we cannot find it, we immediately return to the boat and get the hell out of here. Agree?" Brad asked sternly.

"Agreed. Let's suit up. We need to take both spearguns and extra spears. If it's not dead, it's seriously injured."

The team quickly donned their diving gear, preparing for the potentially dangerous mission ahead. Delgado kept a watchful eye on the surroundings, ensuring the River Queen remained ready for a quick departure if necessary.

With their spearguns and extra spears secured, Alan and Brad slid into the water, their flashlights cutting through the murky depths. They swam towards the spot where the bubbles had stopped, their senses heightened by the tension of the unknown. The shadows of the vegetation in the water playing tricks on them.

As they neared the entrance to the cave where they had found Sarah, the water grew darker and colder, sending a chill through their bones. The once clear river turned into an inky black, an ominous sign of the danger that lurked ahead. Alan signaled to Brad, and with silent nods of understanding, they cautiously left the river and stepped into the cave, their flashlights casting eerie shadows on the rough, jagged walls. The passageway twisted and turned, a labyrinth leading them deeper into the heart of the lagoon, each step echoing with a foreboding sense of unease.

Suddenly, out of the oppressive darkness, the creature emerged with a deafening roar, its eyes blazing with fury. The sight was both terrifying and awe-inspiring, a monstrous guardian of its subterranean realm. It advanced towards Brad and Alan, its movements heavy and labored, but driven by a fierce determination to protect its territory.

Without hesitation, Brad and Alan raised their spearguns and fired, the projectiles piercing the creature's center mass. The beast screamed in agony, a chilling sound that reverberated through the cave. It thrashed wildly, trying in vain to dislodge the spears embedded in its scaly hide.

Adrenaline pumping, Alan and Brad quickly reloaded their spearguns. They aimed and fired again, each shot finding its mark and further weakening the creature. Blood oozed from its wounds, staining the dark water around it.

With a final, guttural roar, the creature collapsed, its massive form falling back into the dark river below the cave entrance. They watched, tense and alert, but the beast did not resurface. The cave grew silent once more, the only sounds the echoes of their breathing and the distant drip of water.

The threat had been neutralized, but the memory of the encounter would haunt them. They knew that the lagoon held many secrets, and the danger was far from over. But for now, they had survived, and Sarah's rescue was a victory in a place where death lurked in every shadow.

Just as they began to congratulate each other, a series of low growls echoed from deeper within the cave. The two froze, listening intently. The sounds grew louder, more distinct, and unmistakably coming from multiple sources.

"What the hell is that?" Brad whispered, his eyes wide with fear.

Alan and Brad exchanged a grim look. "Let's check it out," Alan said, his voice resolute. "We need to know what we're dealing with."

They cautiously ventured back into the cave, their flashlights slicing through the thick darkness. Each step echoed off the damp walls, and the air grew colder as they moved deeper. The low, guttural growls reverberated louder, sending shivers down their spines.

As they turned a corner, their beams of light revealed a scene that made their blood run cold: creatures of various sizes and ages, their eyes glowing with a sinister light, lurked in the shadows. Some were smaller, moving with a predatory grace, while others were larger, their monstrous forms towering over the humans.

Brad and Alan stood frozen in place, the horrifying realization settling in. This wasn't just one rogue creature; it was a thriving colony.

"We need to get the hell out of here," Brad said, his voice shaking with urgency. "Now."

They turned and hurried back towards the entrance, their pace quickening with every step. The growls seemed to follow them, growing louder as if the creatures were aware of their presence and displeased by it.

After a terrifying swim underwater, they burst out into the open air, they sprinted to the River Queen. Brad scrambled aboard while Delgado fired up the engine. The boat roared to life, a comforting sound against the terror that pursued them.

"Did you kill the creature?" Delgado asked, his eyes wide with fear and concern.

"Yes," Brad replied, still panting from the exertion. "But there are more of them. A whole nest. Someone else will have to come back here and take them on."

"Everyone hold on!" Delgado shouted as he steered the boat away from the area, his knuckles white on the wheel.

The River Queen sped through the water, leaving the cave and its horrors behind. The team, though battered and exhausted, felt a wave of relief wash over them. As they put distance between themselves and the Black Lagoon, they couldn't shake the images of the creatures that still lurked in the shadows, waiting.

Their minds raced with the implications of their discovery. The threat wasn't over. It had only just begun. But for now, they were safe, heading towards the first light of dawn and away from the darkness that had nearly consumed them.

CHAPTER 19

The sun hung low on the horizon, casting a warm, golden glow over the River Queen as it gently cut through the dark waters. On deck, and recovering Sarah stood with Emily, Brad, and Alan, their faces lit by the morning light. The air was heavy with a mix of relief and lingering tension, the horrors they had faced still fresh in their minds.

Captain Delgado was in the wheelhouse, his familiar unlit cigar clenched between his teeth as he steered the boat. His eyes, though tired, held a steely resolve, a testament to his years of navigating the treacherous waters of the Amazon.

The four friends stood in silence, each lost in their thoughts. Brad moved closer to Sarah, wrapping his arms around her. She leaned into him, resting her head on his chest, finding solace in the steady rhythm of his heartbeat. Emily and Alan exchanged a glance, their own silent acknowledgment of the bond forged through their shared ordeal.

"We made it," Emily said softly, her voice barely more than a whisper. "We actually made it."

"But at what cost?" Alan replied, his eyes drifting to the dark line of the shore. "The creatures are still out there. The lagoon holds more secrets than we'll ever know."

Brad tightened his embrace around Sarah. "Let someone else figure it out," he said, his voice steady. "For now, we need to focus on recovery and making sure Sarah gets the care she needs."

Sarah looked up at him, her eyes filled with gratitude and something more—a determination to face whatever came next. "We survived," she said, her voice gaining strength. "And we'll keep surviving. Together." Brad kisses her forehead.

The River Queen continued its journey, the familiar hum of the engine a comforting sound in the growing darkness. The boat rocked gently, a soothing contrast to the chaos they had left behind. Captain Delgado glanced back at the group, his gruff exterior softening for a moment as he saw them standing together.

"Hold on tight," he called out, his voice carrying across the deck. "There is a lot of debris in the water. We're not out of the woods yet, but we'll get there."

The boat sliced through the water, leaving a trail of ripples that quickly disappeared in the vast expanse of the lagoon. The sky above was a tapestry of stars, twinkling with a serene indifference to the drama unfolding below.

Emily stepped forward, placing a hand on Alan's shoulder. "We need to make sure this doesn't happen again. We have to tell people what we found. Warn them."

Alan nodded in agreement. "The authorities need to know. Scientists. Anyone who can help us understand what these creatures are and how to stop them."

Brad sighed, looking down at Sarah, then back at his friends. "We will. But first, we need to get back to civilization. Get Sarah to a hospital. Then we can start figuring out how to deal with all this."

Alan goes into the wheelhouse causing Captain Delgado to turn. "Captain. I promised you a bonus if we could get the creature back to civilization."

"I know, Dr. Richards. We tried and failed," Delgado answered.

"No, what I mean is that I still plan on giving you that bonus, but in addition, I would like to give you some funds for the families of Jose and Miguel."

"Gracias, Senor. I'm sure that they families will be most appreciative."

The River Queen pressed on, the afternoongrowing deeper around them. The waters of the Black Lagoon still held their mysteries and dangers, but for now, the team had escaped its grasp. They knew the journey ahead would be difficult, but they also knew they had each other.

As the boat moved steadily forward, Brad, Sarah, Emily, and Alan stood together on deck, a united front against the unknown. The bond they had forged in the face of unimaginable horrors would guide them through whatever challenges lay ahead.

In the wheelhouse, Captain Delgado puffed on his unlit cigar, a faint smile playing at the corners of his mouth. They had survived the Black Lagoon's darkest secrets, and together, they would face whatever came next.

The River Queen sailed into the night, leaving the Black Lagoon behind, but the memories and the promise of more battles to come would stay with them. For now, they had each other, and that was enough.

Bubbles rose ominously from the depths of the Black Lagoon near the cave entrance, breaking the surface in a steady, unsettling rhythm. The dark water rippled, and then, with a splash, an adult creature emerged. Its powerful form glistened in the dim light, and it carried the lifeless body of its kin, spears protruding grotesquely from the corpse.

The creature let out a mournful, enraged roar that echoed through the cave, a primal cry of grief and fury. It carefully laid the body at the entrance of the cave, its glowing eyes filled with a mixture of sorrow and vengeance. The air grew heavy with tension, the lagoon's eerie silence broken only by the creature's ragged breaths.

Shortly, other creatures began to emerge from the shadows, drawn by the call about their fallen comrade. They gathered around the dead creature, their eyes reflecting a savage, collective mourning. Each beast was a testament to the terrifying life that thrived in the hidden depths of the Black Lagoon.

In a sudden, frenzied burst of movement, the creatures descended upon the corpse. Their claws tore into the lifeless body with a brutal efficiency, and their teeth ripped through flesh and bone. The lagoon resonated with the sounds of their feeding, a macabre symphony of crunching and tearing.

The frenzied devouring was more than just sustenance; it was an act of unity, a savage rite that bound them together in their grief and fury. Blood stained the water, turning it into a dark, swirling vortex of red. The creatures' roars and growls filled the air, a stark reminder of the primal, untamed force that lay hidden beneath the lagoon's deceptively calm surface.

As they consumed the remains of their fallen kin, the creatures seemed to grow more agitated, their movements more erratic and violent. The death of one had ignited a fire in their hearts, a collective rage that promised vengeance. Their eyes, glowing with a fierce, predatory light, turned towards the direction where the humans had fled, their intentions clear.

The Black Lagoon, once a mysterious and foreboding place, now pulsed with the raw, unrestrained power of its inhabitants. The creatures, bound by their loss and united in their fury, were ready to defend their domain against any intruders. The waters of the lagoon, now tainted with the blood of the fallen, would remember this day, and so would the creatures.

In the distance, the River Queen sailed towards safety, unaware of the new terror they had unleashed. The creatures watched with a silent, burning resolve, their hunger for revenge as palpable as the darkness that surrounded them. The battle was far from over, and the depths of the Black Lagoon held many more secrets yet to be revealed.

The lagoon's eerie silence returned, but now it was filled with a sense of foreboding, a promise of the violence that was yet to come. The creatures slipped back into the depths, leaving behind only the faint ripples and the memory of their fallen kin.

The Black Lagoon waited, its ancient, dark heart beating with a renewed, terrible purpose.

OTHER BOOKS BY THE AUTHOR:

Horror/Sci fi

House on Haunted Hill Resurrection
The Tingler Unleashed
Beneath the Earth
Carnival of Lost Souls
13 Ghosts Awakened
The Birds Return
The Ice Creature
Wolves of Chernobyl
SEAL: Ghost Recon

Jeannie Loomis Thriller Novels

Ark of the Covenant-Raid on the Church of Our Lady Mary of Zion
Star Chamber
Forgotten Plans
Time Game
Thin Blue Line
The Fourth Reich
Black Heart/Black Cell
The Phantom Train
Rollercoaster
Snow Angel
The Fourth Reich Reborn
Relics of Redemption

Non fiction

Hitting Rock Bottom

Christmas theme

The Hidden Workshop

www.ingramcontent.com/pod-product-compliance
Lightning Source LLC
Chambersburg PA
CBHW020557310726
48979CB00008B/1250/J

* 9 7 9 8 9 9 0 7 2 5 4 7 8 *